BLACK SNOW

A NOVEL BY

ANNE RUSHTON

WHAT IF WE FOUND OURSELVES AT THE MERCY OF NATURE WHEN IT DECIDES TO FIGHT BACK?

BLACK SNOW ... by Anne Rushton

What happens when nature has had enough
of our wasteful, selfish, entitlement attitude
and decides to reclaim the Earth as it once
was ... before pollution,
toxic waste, wanton
destruction?

BLACK SNOW ... by Anne Rushton

Copyright© 2013
ISBN 9780989107280

The following book is a work of fiction.
Any resemblance to actual events or persons ...
living or dead ... is purely coincidental.

PREFACE

THE CLOSE ENCOUNTER

It was New Year's Eve in 2039 while at a friend's party that husband and wife Elliott and Margaret Stewart were making the social rounds when they were approached by Joshua and Janice Adams. They knew them casually and often mingled with them at social events. They hadn't clicked enough to engage them in meaningful conversation or to expand their acquaintance beyond the occasional meetings. After some small talk the Adams said they would like to become better acquainted and invited the Stewarts for mid-afternoon dinner the next day. Everyone slept in and had late breakfast on New Year's Day and a second meal later in the day ... often to the background sound of a football game.

Joshua was a primary care doctor in a large group practice (which was rare in these days ... everyone wanted a specialty) and his wife Janice was a trauma nurse at Jacksonville's largest hospital which appeared to consume her life ... both at the hospital and being on call for mass casualty emergencies. They were approaching middle age just as the Stewarts were.

Elliott and Margaret had been married fifteen years ... she was by then 40; Elliott 43. He was an Adjunct Professor of Meteorology - Climatology at the local University in

Jacksonville, Florida. He was also called in as consultant to NOAA and backup television broadcaster during hurricanes ... of which they were getting more than their share in recent years. When he wasn't involved in teaching, consulting or broadcasting, he was a published writer ... mostly articles in weather and climate periodicals in the academic circles. He wasn't a 'storm chaser' ... that fad had faded during the 2020s when government funding had finally opened up and began feeding money into developing technical equipment and drones which safely tracked storms and other weather issues down to the street level. It was amazing to watch what this high tech equipment could safely capture in real time.

After they all toasted the beginning of 2040 the group began to drift away from the party (the ball drop in Times Square had been discontinued in 2020 when the lovely crystal globe somehow broke free of its mooring, crashed into the crowd, injuring or killing numerous people. The incident was meticulously investigated, but the reason for the mishap was never released despite public demands). Most had almost come to accept this lack of disclosure because over the past decade, the government had made a strong case about combating the continuing battle of terrorism by sequestering certain information for 'national security reasons'. Everyone assumed it was an evil plot which brought death and destruction to Times Square, although none of the known terrorist groups took credit for it, which was a little odd.

BLACK SNOW ... by Anne Rushton

On the short drive home they were both lost in our own thoughts. "Margaret, what do you suppose that was all about? I mean we know Joshua and Janice casually, but why would they want to pursue a friendship with us? Neither Joshua nor Janice have time for canasta parties or fund raisers. You are nearly indispensable as Business Manager at the law firm and you know my schedule works like throwing darts at a dart board."

"Let's just be pleasant and make it a nice afternoon. We know neither of them has time for charity work, so that isn't what this is about. After all, tomorrow is Friday and we can afford some social time with the free weekend coming up. I can't remember when we both had four days running without a work schedule to follow."

They went to dinner the next day ... dutifully impressed by their stunning home ... and spent a surprisingly relaxed afternoon getting to know Joshua and Janice ... or rather them getting to know the Stewarts. On the drive home, Margaret was thinking allowed "Odd how they always kept turning the conversation back toward us. They seemed genuinely interested in getting to know all about every detail of our lives."

CHAPTER 1

Margaret met Elliott in Tucson, Arizona in 2025 shortly after a brief, failed marriage to a forgettable man who was simply not husband material. She and Elliott fell into a nice friendship right away and within the year were married. Nine months later in 2026 Brenda was born. She was the delight of their lives and it seemed life was finally back on track for Margaret. They doted on her and Margaret was more than willing to set her legal career aside to become a full time wife and mother.

Four years after her birth, Brenda became sick and died within a month. Doctors did all they could to treat this 'new and unknown' virus that had been striking children at random. She was the first child in Tucson to die from this and for a time the Stewarts were shunned from the world. For lack of a better term her death certificate stated 'died of viral consumption of unknown origin'. The virus had literally consumed her system before the medical community could do a thing.

They finally elected to remove life support so that her suffering would end. Although Brenda and her parents were quarantined in a private room with its own ventilation system at the hospital, they also didn't want the virus to slither through the halls on a shoe sole and attack some other child or children. As the coroner and doctors came to take her away dressed in their haz mat suits, Margaret lost it completely. This was her precious four year old daughter ...

not a rabid animal they were handling. They carefully wrapped her in sheets and enclosed her in an airtight body bag. Her parents were not even allowed to keep a lock of her hair or attend her memorial service since they remained quarantined for another two weeks. (Brenda's remains were cremated and at some later time her parents were given her ashes in a sealed urn.)

Being at the hospital was in some way a small comfort because they still felt Brenda's presence ... they were grasping at anything to help them make some sense of this tragedy. When they finally went home it was there the brunt of the grief hit them both full force. Although sick, the last time they had been here Brenda was part of this house. Now her room was empty ... totally devoid of furniture, toys, clothes which had been removed for their safety after Brenda died. The medical community had seen this before and it was always 100% fatal but they still didn't have a name for it or any treatment.

In late 2030 ... a few months after Brenda's death ... Elliott returned to his career as a meteorologist for a local television station to distract himself. Margaret had nothing but empty arms and a few pictures to look at. She found herself becoming withdrawn ... a recluse. Not even a teddy bear could be saved ... it was as though Brenda never existed. Trying to be kind and stumbling as people always do, friends and family avoided talking about her for a long time. This made it worse for Margaret ... she wanted to talk

... she had to find an answer that she could live with. She never could ... not then and not now.

After a few months of unrelenting grief, one evening Elliott sat down with Margaret and suggested she return to work. He was trying to be practical and help her rejoin the living, but all she felt was pain ... not just emotional suffering but physical pain all over. She finally agreed to seek some medical help, but not go back to work. Margaret's last job before Brenda's birth had required intense concentration and strict organization ... neither of which she could ever imagine having again.

CHAPTER 2

As the months following Brenda's death dragged on, Margaret allowed a glimmer of hope to return that one day she might actually breathe again. The small glimmer replaced some of the grief. At some point the medication and counseling sessions helped melt some of the brain fog she had carried inside her head. She had focused on nothing in life but trying to understand and make sense of what happened to her baby. Once the fog began to lift and Margaret was able to step away from the continual loop thought process, she began to live without the pain doubling her over.

Over time she came to terms with the idea that Brenda had been the brightest spot ... the pinnacle ... of her life, her love, her achievement, her enrichment. But the spot was gone and would be gone forever. Margaret had to move through life facing forward and not facing backward ... being dragged along into her future unwillingly. She had to replace the grief with something ... anything.

It was during this healing process in early 2031 that Elliott and Margaret received a registered letter from the CDC in Atlanta, Georgia. Neither of them was prepared to see what it contained. The letter began with the obligatory note of condolences ... blah, blah, blah. The next paragraph knocked the wind out of them. A diagnosis had finally been made in Brenda's cause of death from the tissue samples they kept from autopsy in a continuing attempt to identify this new killer of children. Cause of death: 'mutant strain of Hantavirus Pulmonary Syndrome'. The envelope also contained a sealed lock of Brenda's hair which they were assured contained none of the virus ... still it contained the warning 'HERMETICALLY SEALED ... DO NOT ATTEMPT TO OPEN'. They both just stared at it and gently rubbed their fingers over it. While far from closure, they finally had an answer ... and a tangible remembrance of the bright star of their life as a family.

"Margaret, some of the pieces of this puzzle are finally starting to fit together. For years now we have had increasing numbers of Haboob dust storms which have come in from the dry desert and blanketed southern Arizona cities. The meteorological explanation is too complicated to explain now, but these wind storms pick up huge amounts of dry desert dust and sand, build for miles and barrel their way across whatever is in their pathway. It began as a rare phenomenon decades ago, but now they seem to come at will. Weather and climate experts have been trying to figure out the dynamics of what is causing them to appear more often, but so far it's all just conjecture."

"Well, for God's sake Elliott, how could a Haboob kill Brenda?"

"Hantavirus is fairly rare except in vast dry areas where the rodent population is prolific. The virus is carried by a flea from rodent to rodent. No doubt some of the virus was caught up in one of these Haboob dust storms carried over our area, and the dusty fallout contained the virus which killed Brenda."

"But the CDC said 'mutant' ... what does that mean?"

"Viruses have the ability to mutate ... change in some way genetically to better fit its environment or invade a host or avoid annihilation by medicine. One of the mutants could have been in a dust storm which Brenda inhaled. You remember some of the ones we had when she was a toddler ... you insisted on sealing windows and doors to keep the dust out for cleanliness ... I always rinse the car, driveway ... even the house ... just to get rid of the damn stuff ... it is everywhere. It grounds planes and people become reclusive. These storms have become reminiscent of the dust bowl days of the 1930's. Perhaps they come in hundred year cycles ... who knows."

CHAPTER 3

Within a week or two after getting the CDC letter, Elliott came home from work early one day. Now that his research was complete, he was ready to discuss it with Margaret.

"Well, look what the wind blew in early ... you didn't get fired did you?" Margaret was reading a book ... about law ... which Elliott took to be a good omen.

"What would you think about moving across country to Jacksonville, Florida?"

Elliott's question was unexpected and just hung in the air waiting on Margaret's response.

"Have you lost your mind Elliott ... or maybe the dust is getting to you too. This is where we both were raised and spent our adult lives."

"What's to keep us here ... I mean both our parents have died ... and the few siblings we have are scattered to the winds with families of their own."

"Brenda's memory for one thing."

"Margaret, perhaps one of the reasons for leaving here is Brenda's death. These Haboob dust storms continue to blanket the west ... now in New Mexico and west Texas. Every year more people ... now including the old and infirm and folks who are marginalized in society are dying from this virus. I have a theory about that, but my co-workers laugh every time I bring it up. They say it is a freak of nature and will go away on its own."

"You know, we seldom talk about your work because weather is such a boring subject ... OK, what is your theory, Elliott?"

"I think it is the tremendous proliferation of wind farms here in the west. At the turn of the century in 2000, they were still considered a patchwork fix for reducing the carbon footprint ... the ones who were laughing stopped laughing once the experimental wind farms began to show real promise of reducing fossil fuel emissions. Everyone who had a dollar to invest did so in cooperative wind farms. They became the stock market of the west ... and I don't think it was a coincidence that the dust storms started and grew in intensity as the wind farms proliferated."

"Wind farms."

"And it isn't just about the weather ... I think it involves far more than that ... gradual and not so gradual climate change."

"So let me see if I understand ... you want to move to Jacksonville because of wind farms?"

"Margaret, I have an opportunity to become an adjunct professor of meteorology and climatology at a University in Jacksonville ... in addition, part of that package would include consulting with NOAA during hurricane season, AND becoming a backup broadcaster during hurricanes. More and more I find myself immersed in research because of the accelerating rate of climate change ... being part of a

14

University faculty would allow me the access to an endless source of research materials."

"This is the most alive I have seen you Elliott since Brenda died. You must be serious and obviously want to do this."

"Yes and yes Margaret ... do you want to think about making such a move ... just don't take too long because the position needs to be filled by next week before the Atlantic Hurricane Season for 2031 starts June 1 and I have first dibs on the package."

"Well, my wonderful career as mother died with Brenda and you know how I feel about having more children. I couldn't face the possibility of another ride on that emotional roller coaster. In fact, I am not really off the last one. It was so blissful ... and so horrid in the end. I guess the only other thing keeping us here is our home. The real estate market has been depressed for years ... decades really. The crash in 2008 was manmade ... brought on by deregulation, greed, lack of oversight and the explosion of disgusting and illegal financing activity in the years before. Then Wall Street got into the act and there was no way to go but down. Everyone grabbed as much of the financial pie as they could with both hands. Once that bubble burst, the fallout of foreclosure and abandoned housing hit like a cyclone all over the country. Statistics show the western states were hit the hardest, since the housing market had been artificially inflated for decades before the crash. It was the 'perfect storm' of circumstances to all come into play at once. Regardless, we would likely have to take a loss if we sold the house, or worse yet having to lease it out. We own about half the equity here so we could just walk away like so many folks who are under water with their mortgage higher than the value of their property".

"Margaret, those are just mechanics ... let me deal with that. What I am asking you is if you would be willing to move to a new environment, support me in my efforts to try and build another life for us. I would be making substantially more money than here and would be building tenure at the University which would be some security. Who knows, some day I could move up to full professorship or even department head. I love what I do ... I can't imagine doing anything else in my life. It is more than a job ... it is a passion. With the climate changes taking place all over the world, especially in this country, my work will always be in demand ... however long 'always' is."

"Elliott, I really have no reason for staying and you have every reason for wanting to go. Lets do it."

Taking in a deep breath and letting it out slowly, Elliott continued "OK ... Jacksonville is a city nearly twice the size of Tucson in population. It is not in a totally different weather zone ... hot and humid and subject to hurricanes ... which is different from the hot and dry and dusty we have here. It's a coastal city. It's not like moving to Alaska ... the changes would actually be minimal ..."

"Elliott, you are just talking geography ... what do we

16

have to do to get from here to there? Tell me what to do, give me a schedule and I will do anything I can to support you and at least try to help us start over."

"You start packing, sorting out the unnecessary from the necessary ... I think we might just sell the house furnished. I rather not drag any of this dust along with us. Leave the rest to me."

"Sounds fine with me. It will give me something to do and it could be the chain that can pull me out of this living grave I have dug for myself."

Elliott gently embraced Margaret for a long time ... it was his first glimmer of hope they might move forward in a very long time. Near tears, he whispered "I love you Margaret ... you mean the world to me ... you always have ... we have almost forgotten how to be partners. Let's go out to celebrate with dinner and a bottle of good wine."

CHAPTER 4

The game plan was put into motion. Elliott accepted the offer in Florida the next day and they put their home up for sale. He was given a month to close out his life in Tucson and be in Jacksonville. Margaret spent her time cutting ties, gathering moving boxes, making endless lists, phone calls, and deciding what would go and what would be left behind. She was a natural organizer and the more she gave to this project, the more she got out of it in the way of distraction.

They were both shocked when the third Realtor to show their home called to present an offer. They had decided ahead of time to accept whatever it was unless it was insulting. Elliott had realized that there was an intangible to be gained with this move that couldn't be valued in terms of dollars. A new city, a new life, a restart. There are some things you CAN run away from. Memories will always be there but physically separating oneself from the environment in which the bad ones lived can draw a small line in the sand. Never having to pass the hospital where Brenda died ... never passing the school she would have started the following year.

Margaret and Elliott accepted all the terms of the contract and the closing was set for three weeks from that day. There was little time ... or interest ... in celebrating. It was a bittersweet experience and would become more so as moving day approached. Much had to be done. The first order of business would be to fly to Jacksonville and meet his superiors ... both at the University and at NOAA and the local television station. The University had graciously provided them with a furnished apartment on campus they could move to. As they said, "put your things in storage and take your time finding a new home".

They loved Jacksonville with its blue skies, clean air, the constant ocean breeze from the east, the sandy beaches and the Atlantic Ocean which lapped at the city. The people they met were cordial and had a layer of ease that must be a part of what they had heard called the 'Florida Lifestyle'. The city had sprawled itself on the north and south of the St. John's River that had bisected it east from west ... and north from south in places. They were reminded that the hardest part to adapt to would be to learn their directions. Once lost on the east side looking for a location on the west side could involve extra hours and not minutes of backtracking.

Elliott couldn't help but stare at the beauty before him ... lush green lawns, trees, blooming plants ... all pouring out fresh oxygen for him to breathe. All public transportation ran on either hydrogen or electric fuel cells. Traffic gridlock was nowhere to be seen since all the directional signals had become computerized to maximize efficiency. A magnetic levitation train ... a monorail ... had been built in the median of the many interstates cutting thru the city. One of the two beltways around Jacksonville had been built some ten years earlier to eliminate most of the intercity exits, allowing long distance travelers to zip around one side of the city in half the time it took when there were exits every half mile. He loved the innovative approach the city leaders had taken ... and had taken seriously ... to bring Jacksonville into its 'model city' status. Built and retrofitted not only for today, but well into the 22nd century.

Even garbage was modernized and mechanized. Recycling and composting of every bit of reusable waste was mandatory. Separate nonrecycle containers folks still pushed to the curb for pick up were weighed at each stop and customers charged per pound accordingly.

Tucson had made its own strides in moving along these by-now nationally mandated systems, but so much of its funding was being drained away by cleaning up after the Haboobs and retrofitting vehicles, planes and ventilation systems to withstand the dust. No amount of money could be thrown into controlling the dust storms so they had to be endured and cleaned up after. No one could say with any certainty if they were an anomaly or here to stay.

After all the hiring contracts were settled, Elliott and Margaret flew home ... more anxious to move than they dared show. Neither wanted the other to think they were being disrespectful to Brenda's life ... and now memory. If only they could have brought her here with them. No dust there ... just clean air and beautiful fine sand that couldn't hurt anything.

CHAPTER 5

As anxious as Elliott and Margaret were to start a new life, it was still hard to let go of the old one. People are creatures of habit and they were more than a little intimidated by the learning curve they would have to pass through to find the comfort level they had in Tucson. They reminded each other often that they had to pass through this fog of doubt, uncertainty, dread and at times, stark white fear of leaving all they ever knew and move nearly 3,000 miles away to a place they knew practically nothing about. Luckily, they seldom had these seeds of doubt spring to life at the same time. They could each encourage the other ... this was part of their 'new team' as they began to call themselves. All of this was just the 'mechanics' of life and neither of them had ever let the mechanics get in the way of moving a project forward.

It was best to ignore the entire plan and take one step at a time ... not looking for the 'end game' as Elliott came to call it. They would know when they got there ... in the meantime, just keep putting one foot in front of the other. Little wonder they had these emotional moments ... both of them had spent some of the happiest days of their lives in Tucson ... and some of the worst.

The day after they returned from Jacksonville, Elliott gave his official notice at the broadcasting station, although it was not unexpected. He had shared some of this with close co-workers, in particular a few people in the weather department who might take his place. Margaret was well into packing, donating and putting stickers on furniture items to leave so the movers wouldn't take them by mistake. Closets were always the worst ... and hardest places to tackle, and she had left them for last.

The moving van arrived as planned early on Friday afternoon ... after the closing of their house sale that morning. Everything had gone smoothly at the closing which is always a relief to all parties. So many times there are last minute snags that have to be unsnarled and could delay closings for hours or even days. None of that here ... all parties knew their job and did it well ... relieving Elliott and Margaret of that worry.

Once packed of mainly boxes and cardboard clothing closets, the van driver had them sign some papers, recheck their destination location, and closed the door of the van which contained all their worldly possessions. He reminded them it would be a week ... give or take a day ... before he arrived in Jacksonville since he had two more stops along the way. The van was enormous and could carry the contents of four small homes ... each segregated in its own steel compartment. Loading and unloading was done from the side of the truck, so as not to co-mingle contents from other homes.

This part of the plan was over and it was time for Elliott and Margaret to take their final walk thru of the rooms ... some got a quick glance ... others they walked through carefully ... touching drapery, the walls, looking out the

BLACK SNOW ... by Anne Rushton

windows at the familiar views, tearfully taking a picture of the growth chart inside of Brenda's closet they had marked every six months of her short life. Margaret had wanted to cut out that piece of the door trim and take it ... surely it wouldn't be missed by the new owners once the closet was filled with toys and clothing belonging to their own daughter. Elliott said they should leave it intact. As hard as it was to walk away from that reminder, that was the very reason to leave it. While Brenda would live in their memories and hearts forever, the farther they moved away from her death in time ... and miles ... the more tolerable the pain would become. He reasoned if they took the piece of wood, every time they saw it the scab on their wounds would be opened. They closed the door to the house and turning around once more to sear the picture into their memory, they drove away.

CHAPTER 6

As they had planned at the closing, they met the new owners for dinner and to hand over the keys. The restaurant the new owners chose was one Elliott and Margaret had never been to for good reason. The four of them had become friends during the past few weeks and knowing the Stewarts' story, the buyers wanted to go to a new place to represent a new beginning for them all.

They waited for their reservation to be called and spent the brief time congratulating each other on a 'new life'. Once seated the buyers ordered a bottle of champagne to toast the occasion. To fill the empty air, they inquired what arrangements had been made about their vehicles since Elliott and Margaret would be spending the night at a local hotel and flying to Jacksonville the next morning.

"Considering the cost of cars now, and the fact ours were fairly new and exactly what we wanted, we decided it would be more economical to ship the two of them by rail rather than sell them here and buy new in Jacksonville. Brenda's favorite color was blue, so Margaret bought an inside and outside powder blue car and didn't want to let it go. We have a rental now and will turn it in before we leave. We have a rental reserved on the other end."

"Seems like you two have covered all ... um ... as many bases as you could. We promise to take good care of your ... um ... our lovely home. During our last walk through inspection we saw the growth chart you had kept inside your daughter's closet. Rest assured we will never paint over it and we will always keep that room in some shade of blue."

Margaret's eyes filled with unexpected tears as she whispered a heartfelt "thank you for the kindness you have shown us during this trying ordeal". She felt Elliott's hand squeeze hers under the table.

After dinner, their last piece of business was to hand over the keys. The four parted company, each biding a fond farewell with best wishes for the future.

By the time they checked into their hotel, Margaret felt herself shift into auto pilot. Perhaps it was exhaustion, perhaps it was a defense mechanism, perhaps it was just all too much to process ... maybe it was all of it.

CHAPTER 7

The following morning they stepped aboard the plane which would take them from their world to a new life. After they were aloft Margaret looked out the window for one last look of Tucson. As it disappeared from view, she doubted she would ever see it again. She had the only things with her that made life worth pursuing ... Elliott and Brenda's ashes.

After landing in Jacksonville, they picked up their rental car and headed for another hotel near the airport. They were running on fumes ... physically and emotionally ... but part of their exhaustion this night was from anticipation of what was to come. Each day and night took them one step closer to a new life. Following dinner ordered from room service, they both fell asleep ten minutes into a movie they ordered.

The following morning, Sunday, they slept until noon, more exhausted than they imagined. They had run on full throttle during the month between Elliott's announcement of this offer and actually laying in the hotel bed. They luxuriated by ordering a late breakfast from room service.

"Well, my dear wife, what would your pleasure be for the afternoon?"

"I think I would really like to go to the beach and sink my toes in the sand ... something that wouldn't be like a layer of mud. Now Elliott just how do beach people manage that?"

"Manage what?"

"It's like which came first the chicken or the egg. You sit on the beach, get covered with sand, go down to the ocean to rinse off, walk back up the beach to the car where you get covered in sand again."

"Do you want a practical answer or something silly?"

"Silly."

"You do it one step at a time."

"Why didn't I see that coming."

"Hey lady, you opened the door; I just walked through it." They both laughed ... then giggled ... then laughed again and for so long and so loud they snorted orange juice out their noses ... which made laughing more uncontrollable. When they finally got themselves under control, they realized what a sense of relief they felt by letting their raw emotions just take over and vent.

After their trip to see the beautiful Atlantic Ocean and it's rhythmic lapping waves move up and down the beach ... as the waves had done for eons ... they felt somehow renewed. "This is therapy Elliott. Whenever we need some inner peace and calm, this is where we should come. It seems to put things in order for me and helps me see life based on what I would call the 'grand scheme of things'. I never lived near enough to the ocean that I could just drop by for an afternoon. Now I understand part of its lure. It is so enormous and we are so infinitely small. The ocean and the life it supports goes on and on and on ... meeting challenges, overcoming disasters like hurricanes, healing itself of the wounds inflicted on it and the life it supports. I need to do that too."

BLACK SNOW ... by Anne Rushton

Elliott suggested they find a seafood restaurant with a table outside facing the water. In one brief afternoon, he had seen a change in Margaret ... for the better ... he, too, felt a sense of serenity. He made a mental note to consider buying a house or condo with an ocean view.

The next day they moved what little they brought with them on the plane ... two large suitcases each ... to the apartment the University had offered them. It was far more than either of them expected. While it didn't have an ocean view, it did have a water view ... the St. John's River which crisscrossed Jacksonville in several places. The decor was pure Florida ... rattan, bamboo, a lot of soft muted colors. It was very tastefully done Margaret thought as she moved from one room to another. She counted two master bedrooms with attached baths, several walk-in closets and one very large room with living room, dining area and kitchen all carefully laid out to separate their uses by furniture and floor coverings. The entire apartment was painted the color of burlap and had stark white tile. The bedrooms and baths were accented with a seafoam blue-green, and the great room was accented in a very pale peach shade. It was a very calming environment.

"You know Elliott, I think I could just live here and be happy, but I know the University keeps it for guests or folks like us. There isn't a speck of dust anywhere and everything seems to have been chosen at the same time in one store. If just seems 'fresh' and created for comfort."

"Make some notes of what you like about it and when we get to the point of finding our own place, we can look for something similar. We can unpack our suitcases later, but now we better go to the train depot and start the process of picking up our two cars and return the one we rented."

"Elliott, how are we going to do that?"

He could barely get the words out for laughing ... "one step at a time".

CHAPTER 8

As lovely as the apartment was, Margaret couldn't see herself just idling away her time there. They came to Jacksonville to start a new life. Getting this far was only half of it. After Elliott left for work the next day she decided to move toward the second phase of finding a permanent home for themselves. Perhaps then she could focus on herself.

One of the Dean's staff members had sincerely offered to serve somewhat like a concierge for them so she called Evelyn to ask for help. They agreed to meet for lunch at the small restaurant in their apartment building. Evelyn said she would bring a lot of information with her that might help in her house search.

After the meeting Margaret had enough to study for the rest of the afternoon. She was grateful Evelyn had been so helpful about different parts of Jacksonville ... Margaret didn't want to live in a high rise condominium or in an area of transient tourists. Neither she nor Elliott were interested in golf or tennis, around which so many of the developments had been built. What she really wanted was a small place that had some view ... even a sliver of it ... of the ocean or St. John's River which snaked its way for five miles through the city. At some point Margaret envisioned herself going to work, so she didn't want to live far out to put both her and Elliott into commuting.

Someone from the University had stocked their kitchen well, so when Elliott came in about six she had dinner ready.

BLACK SNOW ... by Anne Rushton

She looked forward to spending time that evening talking about his day ... and her day. Elliott was so enthusiastic with details of his work, she didn't think they would ever get around to 'her day'.

Elliott started to wind down after an hour or so, so she approached him with her day's work. It really hadn't been work ... it kept her engaged all day and she was even beginning to feel enthusiastic about house hunting.

"This is great Margaret ... I am so glad you took the initiative so soon to start looking for a place to live."

"What we really need to do Elliott is to narrow down first what section of the city we want to live in and what we both want in a house. Evelyn gave me a city map and diagramed it to show the type of housing found in different areas. I really don't want to live in a condo, or in a transient tourist area, or a sports development, so I have crossed off those areas of Jacksonville. I don't think we either want to live outside the city for commuting purposes, and I know you want to be as close to the University as possible. Once we have chosen a few areas to look in, we need to decide on a budget and the specific things we are looking for in a home. Evelyn circled in blue the areas she thought would be suited to our needs."

Elliott set his wine glass down and leaned over to look at the map Margaret had laid out on the coffee table. "It looks to me like she has done half our work for us ... so nice of her ... I will have to remember to thank her in person and put in a good word with the Dean ... that is, if I ever just run into him in a hallway! You wouldn't believe how enormous that campus is ... it will take me weeks just to learn my way around and find the best route to my office ...".

He could tell by the look on Margaret's face that his time limit for work talk was up so he rerouted the conversation back to the house hunt. "Did Evelyn suggest any Realtors we might contact?"

"She gave me a list of names of Realtors who worked each of the areas she outlined in blue. She said they had all helped faculty members find housing, so they knew where to look."

At Margaret's suggestion they each made a list of 'must haves' and 'deal breakers'. When they compared the two, Margaret laughed out loud. She had gone into great detail on her list of paper, almost filling it. Elliott wrote under 'must haves' a roof with four walls and water view; his 'deal breakers' were a roof with four walls and no water view'.

Afraid she would start snorting out wine from her nose, Margaret set her glass down before letting out a belly laugh. God, it felt so good to have something to make me laugh again, she thought to herself.

"Margaret you are much better than I am at this ... whatever and wherever it is, we will make it a lovely home. I want it to be a place where you walk in and think 'this is the real deal'."

BLACK SNOW ... by Anne Rushton

After they worked out a budget she put the papers away. She actually felt good about herself and was looking forward to the task at hand. Elliott had given her nearly 'carte blanche' ... so except for location and budget, she could choose any home she fell in love with. Being the practical person she was, Elliott had no concern that Margaret would be swept away by the Realtors or lured into a listing they could not afford or didn't need.

CHAPTER 9

Once Margaret actually began the house hunt, it didn't take long for her to realize that life in Jacksonville was going to be far different than Tucson. Not just the weather difference and not just the fact they would be living in a coastal city. The house styles were different and the prices were higher than Tucson. In Arizona the census figures had shown a net loss of residents caused by more people moving out than in. She hadn't realized until just then how lucky they were to have sold their home in Tucson so quickly.

She had talked with several Realtors ... interviewed actually ... and had narrowed it down to one who had impressed her the most. Andrea Bivens came to visit her the day after Margaret had called to engage her services. She guided Margaret in accessing a personal list of prospective homes on the electronic tablet she brought with her. Using Margaret's specifications, Andrea had narrowed down her selections to a dozen and felt sure the Stewarts would find one of them suitable for their needs. "Keep this tablet to study and discuss the listings with Elliott tonight. Message me with the ones you want to see in the order of desirability and I will make arrangements for a personal viewing tomorrow." When Andrea picked Margaret up early the next day the Realtor assured her any of the listings she chose would be a good selection and off they went.

By lunchtime Andrea had shown Margaret four listings. They stopped to eat and Margaret told her she didn't want or need to see anymore. After taking a 360° virtual tour of the properties the night before, Margaret had all but decided on the one she wanted provided the walk thru went well. It had.

Within two weeks, the Stewarts were proud homeowners. As they left the closing, both of them felt like things were falling into place on which to build a solid future. They could hardly wait to retrieve their things from storage and move in. As Elliott suggested, they had sold their Tucson home furnished, so Margaret had some serious furniture shopping to do before they could actually live in their new home..

Andrea had been a tremendous help with that too, putting Margaret in touch with a decorator who could guide her along the way. She and Elliott had never lived in what she would call a 'grownups' house ... one to not only live in but to entertain the few friends they had made thus far, and reciprocate dinner invitations from the faculty ... and in time to host their own parties.

Margaret and Elliott continued living on campus at their University-provided apartment until everything at their new house was move in ready. Their boxes from Tucson were retrieved from storage and unpacked, new furniture set in place amid the sophisticated decor the decorator had suggested, and the only thing left to do was walk thru the front door. Elliott took note of what a symbolic event it was to turn the key in the front door, which in many ways was like turning a key in the door which would open into a new future

BLACK SNOW ... by Anne Rushton

for them.

CHAPTER 10

At the end of her first marriage and before she married Elliott, Margaret had graduated from law school. She wanted a breather from academics and delayed taking the bar exam. Then she and Elliott were married, Brenda came along and Margaret was 'mother-in-charge' for the four delightful years she had her. To sit for the bar exam then would require no less than a year of study, catching up and preparing herself mentally. There was also the stress issue to consider. Margaret was just beginning to come back into the sunlight and knew she was not in any condition to endure the bar.

She was a lawyer ... her diploma said she had earned her Juris Doctorate ... but she couldn't practice law without a license and couldn't get a license without passing the bar. She had the knowledge, the organizational skills, and she desperately needed an intense distraction. Margaret decided to market herself as a business manager to a medium sized law firm, of which there were many, in Jacksonville. She reasoned that she wouldn't have to endure the hideous hours of drudge work that many new attorneys have to go through to prove their worth. She wouldn't have to compete to become an 'Associate' as in 'John Doe & Associates' on the letterhead. She wouldn't have to work herself half into the grave to claw her way into becoming a 'Partner'.

When Margaret shared her thoughts with Elliott, he was very happy and said he was very proud of the way she had analyzed the situation, identifying her strong points and being able to pull together what she could offer.

It seemed a good plan. Much to her surprise, once she prepared her resume, a statement of personal work ethics and list of qualities she could bring to the table without having to be paid a practicing attorney's salary, Margaret received a warm reception at three of the six firms she interviewed with. Two actually called her back in to offer her a 'package', one of which she accepted. Margaret allowed herself a brief moment of self satisfaction and could hardly wait to tell Elliott.

"I am very proud of you Margaret ... not because you are going to work or adding to the cash flow, but that you made a concerted effort to rejoin life. So happy you want to do something on your own, instead of just being on the sidelines. Whatever happens with this job doesn't matter ... it is the 'taking the first step' that is the hardest and most important. The one thing I don't want is to see you walk into a lot of stress or pressure ... or deadline work ... or crazy people making demands of you."

"I appreciate your kind words Elliott ... I really do hope it works out. I didn't do this because I felt I should do it, or that I needed a diversion or distraction ... I really wanted to be a part of something important that I could make a contribution to."

CHAPTER 11 ... 2032

The night before the first day at her new job Margaret allowed herself some quiet time of introspection. It was safer now to think of some of the bad parts of her life because by then there was the counter balance of hope. It seemed like the last leg of a long journey to her. She and Elliott had grieved so after Brenda's death and she didn't think life would ever hold anything of interest ever again. At Elliott's urging they had left Arizona in 2031 ... it seemed like years ago instead of months ... and moved to Jacksonville to take advantage of a wonderful career opportunity for Elliott. She had no reason to stay in Tucson and no reason to move to Florida ... no reason for doing much of anything. She didn't want to become a hindrance to Elliott's advancement ... especially in a career he was so passionate about. She had forced herself into a position of support for him and that seemed to lay the groundwork for her own rebirth in life.

Finding, buying, furnishing and decorating a new home for them also forced her to engage life and have a million things to think about other than the devastation in her life in Tucson when Brenda died. It pleased her when Elliott took special note of something she had added to their home, or the color she had painted a room. She knew they would never have anymore children, so she didn't need to 'child-proof' anything. She allowed her fanciful nature to blossom at the new house ... especially in the landscaping. Such stunning choices she had now. She wanted one of everything at the plant stores the landscape designer took her to. While Jacksonville did not lay in the 'tropical' or even 'semi-tropical' zone, it was still in Florida and she wanted a total change from the near barren landscape, the drought and dust storms she endured in Tucson. 'Jungle' is what she envisioned ... and 'jungle' is what she got. She was in love with her home, in love with the view of the St. John's River a block away, and except for that corner of her heart that would never be repaired, she had rejoined life as much as she could.

CHAPTER 12

Margaret took special note of the building she was about to enter in downtown Jacksonville. It fit well among the other low rise buildings in that part of the city ... she thought of it as 'classic business' ... or 'understated elegance'. A very tasteful wooden sign on the wall near the door said it all ... 'Woodward, Woodward & Associates, Attorneys-At-Law' along with the address. Margaret was pleasantly greeted by a receptionist who introduced herself as Grace Morgan. Grace was expecting her and let James Woodward, Sr. know she had arrived. While they waited, Margaret and Grace exchanged pleasantries of the day. Margaret was not really good at that ... once she entered the 'arena' as she called it, she was all business even on the first day. It was just a part of who she was.

"Welcome Margaret. I do hope you will enjoy your work here. We can certainly use someone to keep us organized. Often times I feel like I am trying to herd cats."

Margaret laughed and replied "I look forward to being of some use to you, the firm and myself."

"Let me show you to your room. I am the old man of the group, James Woodward, Sr. ... everyone just calls me 'Senior' to distinguish me from my partner and son, James Woodward, Jr. who we all call 'Junior'. I have called a staff meeting for 10 this morning in the law library just for the purpose of introducing you. As customary, we all wear a name tag for the first two weeks anyone new comes aboard, except in the presence of clients, of course."

Margaret thought to herself 'so far, so good ... now let's get down to the reason I am here'. She was pleased with the office they had made ready for her by transferring its last occupant to the second floor. She was sure whoever that was had not been pleased with the move and word would filter down to her eventually as to who had been uprooted. The sign on her desk said 'Margaret Stewart, Business Manager and Research Specialist'. She was pleased with that and before she could stop herself, uttered aloud "and herder of cats". Senior laughed and seemed to enjoy her sense of humor.

"Senior, the first thing I would like to have is a detailed job description to know exactly what you expect of me so that I might budget my time wisely. The second thing that would be most helpful is a detailed floor plan of the practice so I don't have to keep interrupting someone asking directions."

"Margaret, I knew by our interview how well organized you were with your thoughts, so I am ahead of you. You will find both of those items in your top center drawer. Any questions ... and you shouldn't be embarrassed to ask ... my para legal Auburn can answer ... she has been with me fifteen years and sometimes I think she knows more about this business than I do. I will get back to work and see you at ten."

Margaret sat down in the oversized arm chair and began looking at the written instructions for new employees regardless of their capacity. An account had been set up for her on the computer and she began filling in tax information. She silently thanked President Nelson for overcoming six years of opposition during her presidency to finally have the old tax code abolished and a new one set up which all but eliminated laborious tax returns. A sales tax of 10% across the board for everyone had replaced not only individual Federal Income Tax, but many other taxes as well. It had all but eliminated accountants whose sole function was to prepare annual tax returns, but so be it ... it was for the 'common good' as the President had put it. It had leveled the playing field for all citizens and was another rung in the ladder of recreating the middle class.

At ten Margaret entered the library and was pleased to see so many smiling faces staring at her. Just as Senior had promised, they all wore name tags. Altogether there was Senior, Junior, eight Associates, fifteen support personnel ranging from the receptionist to legal secretaries to legal assistants to para legals, a bookkeeper ... and her. After she was introduced by name, title, background and job description by Senior, everyone filed out past her, shook her hand and said 'welcome'.

With that over Margaret was back at her desk reviewing her job description. She had been promised a transition period of three days to orient herself before her actual work would begin. She started by finding the supply room on the map and using one of the carts there to stack paper, a box of empty file folders, Will jackets, letterhead and other miscellaneous items. She was required to enter all the items she took on her computer account ... which kept a current running inventory of supplies. Once an item was reduced to a certain level, reordering was done automatically by the computer program. Here again, the computer had eliminated the need for a Stock Clerk ... which would be hard to justify in a small firm like this anyway.

Her focus was so intense and concentration level so perfected that she had to be reminded it was the end of the work day. She had grazed on fruit and cheese brought from home instead of taking a formal lunch hour. Margaret could hardly believe it was 5 o'clock already.

CHAPTER 13 ... 2034

During the two years since Margaret re-charted her own course and began emerging from under the dark cloud that had draped itself over her life so long, Elliott felt he had more time to devote to his passion of studying climate change. He continued his zigging and zagging among Adjunct Professor, working with NOAA on an 'as needed' basis, and supplementing the staff of weather broadcasters during hurricane season. His main interest was in research and publishing his findings.

Elliott's attention was constantly being diverted by unique new weather related events in the world, most particularly in this country and his publishing efforts increased accordingly. He was taken by surprise when the 'search committee' at the University bypassed their usual protocol of advertising for a position of full time professor in his department, and approached him directly with an offer to fill an upcoming vacancy.

"This is quite an honor and vote of confidence you have shown in me and my work. I was unaware of the pending vacancy, so I am taken by complete surprise by your offer. I won't deny that an adjunct professor feels somewhat like a substitute teacher by filling in when the teacher is unavailable. I also won't deny that I think it is the hope of most or many such adjuncts to have their work deemed credible enough over time to be offered the position of full professor. I have no hesitation in accepting your offer and will make myself available to your committee at your convenience to discuss the details. One stipulation I do have is that I am allowed to continue research and writing."

The Dean of the University was obviously pleased with their selection when he said "we wouldn't have expected anything less from you. One concern we have is your relationship with the local broadcasting station. We would like to suggest you back away from that in order to devote your full attention and energy to the University. As for your association with NOAA, we feel your work with them is a very important link to what you can offer your students.

"Your research and writing has gained wide attention in the weather world, and whether you realize it or not, your work and name have come to our attention more than a few times. Our Professor had gained tenure and the only way we could replace him was through his retirement. He indicated his intentions to do so a week or so ago and frankly, your name was first in all our minds to take his place."

Elliott nodded his head in the affirmative and said "agreed on all accounts. Thank you for the vote of confidence". After the group left he felt like dancing around his desk ... he could barely contain his excitement and couldn't wait to tell Margaret. Mostly, it was the affirmation he had received that his work was credible and being taken seriously.

CHAPTER 14 ... 2037

During the intervening three years as Professor, Elliott and Margaret luxuriated in a routine and somewhat uncomplicated life. They had enjoyed all that Jacksonville and coastal living provided. Often invited to social occasions, their network of friends and colleagues far exceeded what they had in Tucson. At times it became a juggling act to decide which activities to take part in. Their life was fuller than it needed to be, but Elliott reasoned that was better than the dark days in Tucson. Dark in more ways than one ... Brenda's death and the dust storms which continued to roll over the far west with greater frequency. He sometimes wondered how people coped there and why they stayed. He knew the answer to that ... which was the same answer to so many other questions of why people tolerate the intolerable. They become so focused on the minutia of day-to-day life ... what he called the pursuit of trivia ... that they don't have the time or wherewithal to raise their heads above it and study the grand scheme.

As bad as the environment was in the west ... not only the dust storms, but the raging mountain fires further polluting the air and suffocating the environment ... they knew what to expect and somehow had learned to cope. Often people are afraid of anything having to do with the unknown like moving away ... even if the unknown held more promise for a better life.

During Commencement ceremonies in May of 2036

BLACK SNOW ... by Anne Rushton

Elliott had been awarded an honorary doctorate degree at the University for his knowledge of, and dedication to, the field of meteorology. His research and writing, which had been sought for publication in academic literature, had by then found its way into mainstream media. More and more, he was being contacted for speaking engagements or interviews which he almost always declined for lack of time. In actuality, he felt trapped between the door of knowledge and the door of alarm. More and more, mainstream America was taking note of the bizarre weather patterns ... or lack of any pattern ... and the topic of weather had become the latest 'fad' interest.

In early 2037, Elliott received a hand delivered registered letter with no return address on it. He debated opening it, but curiosity got the best of him and he carefully slid the letter opener across the top of the envelope. He peeked in to see a letter with FEMA on the letterhead. He reached in immediately and pulled the contents out at once.

The Federal Emergency Management Agency had for many years coordinated disaster relief efforts. While there were many events going on across the country which qualified for their help, he wasn't aware of a disaster on the scope of Hurricane Katrina or Super Hurricane Sandy looming on the horizon.

BLACK SNOW ... by Anne Rushton

"January 10, 2037

Dear Professor Stewart:

It has come to our attention that you are a leader in your profession of meteorology and climatology. Your knowledge and experience could contribute greatly to a conference FEMA and the Department Of Homeland Security is having in early March, 2037 regarding global warming, in particular as it relates to climate change. Your travel to and from Washington, DC, and full accommodations while you are here will be provided by our Department.

The conference will be composed of members of FEMA, NOAA and experts like yourself in the field of weather and climate, leaders in the areas of environment, hydrology, science and medical personnel.

If you are able to attend, we expect you to be prepared to present and read a paper concerning your area of expertise, in particular as it relates to climate change. We would also expect you to participate in general discussion groups.

We await your response by telephone.

> *Respectfully,*
> *Katherine Hobbs, PhD*
> *Director of FEMA"*

BLACK SNOW ... by Anne Rushton

Enclosed with the letter was a hand written card signed by Dr. Hobbs giving Elliott a secured phone number. After some consideration, he called and acknowledged receipt of the letter, verified his identification and accepted their invitation. Elliott was told to expect another registered letter within a week with the details of his flight, accommodations, and the meeting schedule. He could hardly wait to begin work on the paper he would present. No doubt some of his work and writings had reached beyond academics and the average reader. This was a signal that he was being observed by higher authorities in the real world.

As he sat back in his comfortable leather chair, now perfectly conformed to his years of use, it gave him an unexpected sense of dread. While he believed whole heartedly in his research and the findings it produced, in a sense it was confirmation that others were of similar belief ... that the rate of natural weather related disasters was increasing at an alarming rate and had been for several decades. The question he was always left with was what could be done to avert a true natural, national disaster ... the likes of which had not been seen or felt since perhaps what the historians refer to as 'abrupt climate change' some 8000 years ago give or take several decades.

It was one thing to come up with the questions and theories ... quite another to provide the answers. Perhaps this meeting in March would be a start. Perhaps not ... his worst fear was that it would just turn into so much rhetoric

BLACK SNOW ... by Anne Rushton

without any consensus or direction.

CHAPTER 15

As planned, when Elliott arrived at the airport in March of 2037, he was met by an escort dressed in very casual attire. Elliott had been asked to dress in casual attire upon his arrival and to bring casual clothes for the duration. He found it strange they did not choose one of the major airports which served DC, but rather Dulles which was the most remote located in northern Virginia.

He had calmed himself as much as he could during the flight, knowing this meeting was not only the high point of his professional career, but the message he was delivering ... and probably the others ... was a somber one. He was going to walk a delicate tightrope ... hoping not to be received as an alarmist yet taken seriously enough to make a difference. Regardless, he would have a vocal forum and his words would no doubt raise some eyebrows at the very least.

Lost in his own thoughts and rereading the paper he was presenting, Elliott failed to notice the driver was taking him farther away from the city and by then they were in a rural area. "Excuse me sir, are we lost?"

"No sir, we will arrive shortly."

The miniature GPS which doubled as a watch he always wore on his left wrist indicated they had been traveling northwest for an hour. He knew they had crossed the Maryland State Line some time ago ... then it hit him like the proverbial ton of bricks ... Camp David ... the Presidential Retreat. Why not ... important people were attending this conference and where else could the group meet safely in seclusion without interruption and not have any travel between hotels and a meeting place.

They started up a slight incline into a heavily wooded area, then passed through gates which opened automatically at their approach. The gates closed behind them and Elliott saw that they were enclosed on all four sides by steel fence with security cameras posted on the four corners. The driver exited the car, presented himself for scanning, gave a fingerprint and an eye scan. One of the solid iron gates ahead of the car swung open just wide enough for them to pass. Overhead Elliott heard the sound of a helicopter taking off ... was it picking up or dropping off someone? He entertained the ridiculous thought of taking some pictures with his phone, but had to slap himself back to reality. This development really tightened the screws ... he knew by then that it was serious business he was about to engage in.

"Welcome to Camp David Elliott ... you don't mind being called by your first name do you?"

He nervously shook his head. All he could think of was a line from a Broadway musical years ago ... 'if they could see me now ... that old gang of mine ...'. Oh Elliott, he though, you better dig real deep and pull out every manner you ever had ... every ounce of confidence you can muster. This is the 'real deal' ... don't screw it up.

Elliott had been given a schedule for the day upon his arrival, and also a sheet entitled 'House Rules'.

BLACK SNOW ... by Anne Rushton

After being shown to his room, he plopped on the bed and gave himself a stern talking to. Before today he felt at ease in his world of academia, confident he could walk his way past any hurdle. He was, after all by then a full Professor, had been received well in the scientific circles, and everything in his life seemed to have brought him to this very spot. He had what it took to pull it together and pull it off ... he just wasn't sure he knew where 'it' was at that moment.

He immediately dismissed the childlike notion to call Margaret and say 'guess where I am!' Instead he read the House Rules which sounded like he was being sequestered at a military site ... which in some ways this was. He didn't like leaving his cell phone and ear bud at the door as he entered ... or his GPS/watch either. In effect he was virtually cut off from civilization ... but at the same time probably at the safest place in the country.

CHAPTER 16

Elliott looked at the floor plan of this building posted on the wall in his room and found his way to the dining room for a buffet lunch served at noon. A badge awaited him at an empty seat with his name and position printed on it. As he ate, he glanced around the large room and counted a dozen people eating. He could have kicked himself for not doing some research on the FEMA and Homeland Security directors ... they were here he felt sure, but he didn't recognize any faces.

Just then a woman's hand shot out from across the table. "Welcome, I am Susan Lazenby, Director of the Department Of Homeland Security. You must be Dr. Elliott Stewart from Jacksonville. Don't worry, I'm not a mind reader ... I saw your name badge before you sat down."

Elliott regained the breath he had knocked out of him, pulled himself together and decided to play it straight down the middle by following whatever lead he was given. "Thank you for inviting me. I have to say I was surprised and duly impressed to realize my final destination would be Camp David."

Dr. Lazenby responded "Good choice wouldn't you say?"

Elliott nodded and answered "Excellent" without any further comment.

The afternoon meeting began promptly at 2:00 P.M. in an adjoining room. The chairs were set out in a horseshoe configuration, with a podium at the open end. Each chair had a small table in front of it which held a small pitcher of water and ice, a cup, a notepad and a pencil. As he looked for his table, he noticed the Surgeon General's name and position noted on one of the cards.

Dr. Lazenby stepped to the podium and introduced herself. The room was equipped with perfect acoustics and telecoil technology so neither she nor anyone else needed a microphone. After the routine welcome and introduction of the guests, she began to speak.

"Everyone on the Earth lives in an imperfect world ... some places more so than others. What might be surprising to learn is just how imperfect our world is ... in particular America. We are the most industrialized society history has ever recorded ... yet we are one of the most destructive and selfish. I don't mean you and I ... but rather as a whole society one might say. We have raped our land, sucked up our natural resources with the biggest straw we could find, and have gone through life with a catcher's mitt on both hands. AND we have been doing this for over two hundred years.

"All of you here today know why you were asked to come. I won't say 'invited' because that suggests something like a tea party or a wedding. To be brief and to the point, we all started hearing about our 'carbon footprint' well before the 21st century began. A few environmentalists listened ... the government gave lip service by setting up some committees to study global warming ... the rest of us turned a deaf ear so we could just get back to the business of living day-to-day.

"As time passed, wise people began to jump onto the environmental bandwagon. For the most part, no one recognized the names of the advocates until Al Gore spoke up and tried to warn people of what was happening ... and had been happening since the industrial revolution in this country. He was not taken seriously ... and the more he spoke out the more ridicule he received. The sad fact of the matter is that we have now in 2037 just perhaps nearly reached the end of the line of what nature will take from us before really fighting back in ways we may not be able to either control or recover from.

"It is with personal pleasure and a sense of sorrow to introduce our first and only outside speaker at this conference ... pleasure because he bravely took a stand, and sorrow because it appears now he was right all those years ago. Please welcome former Vice-President Al Gore."

The group broke into a spontaneous standing ovation and Elliott was left dumbfounded. This is major serious, he thought to himself.

CHAPTER 17

Following the twenty minute speech by the former Vice-President, Dr. Lazenby resumed her place at the podium.

"The group gathered here today has been called for the sole purpose of presenting their theses on the climate situation. We will proceed with as many presentations as time will allow. Tomorrow morning we will finish that portion of our agenda. After lunch we will begin our roundtable discussions of what ... if anything we can do ... to stop the deterioration. The day after tomorrow we will resume our discussions. You will be our guests that night and free to meet your travel obligations the following morning.

"Our first speaker will be Dr. Elliott Stewart. Dr. Stewart has devoted his professional life to research and publication. He is the Professor of Meteorology and Climatology at the University in Jacksonville, Florida. Under him are three Assistant Professors. Over recent years, their jobs have been to relieve Dr. Stewart of much of his teaching duty so he can work with NOAA and continue his research. Dr. Stewart if you will, you may speak while seated ..."

Elliott was caught off guard being the first to hold court with the dignitaries in the room, and also to follow the former Vice-President's speech which had captivated this captive audience. Dr. Lazenby sat down and Elliott realized his entire career was on the line here ... as well as his credibility. He composed himself and began to deliver what he felt like was a death sentence to a Court defendant.

"For some years my research has convinced me that climate change is upon us in a major way and that it would impact our year round weather the likes of which no one in recorded history had ever experienced. I am not happy to have been proven right. When I say 'climate change' I am not just talking about 'global warming' ... but total climate change in many parts of the world which have been and will continue to cause death, destruction and a complete realignment of resources.

"Just within the past five years we have had unrelenting dust storms in the west, unstoppable forest fires in the far west because of historic level drought, tides reaching record levels on all coastal areas due to glacial melt, more tornadoes, hurricanes in places they never appeared before. Remember the Superstorm Hurricane Sandy on the northeastern corridor of this country in 2012? It was catastrophic ... took years to recover the infrastructure and housing, and it redrew the coastal map of several states. They tried to reassure people by calling it a hundred year storm. Well, it wasn't.

"Sandy was just the start. During late 2013, the Philippines were all but decimated by the strongest typhoon in recorded history. That kind of storm has happened at least once every five years, give or take since then, in places we once thought were immune to hurricanes such as Oregon and Washington state.

BLACK SNOW ... by Anne Rushton

"California has had repeated small earthquakes along the San Andreas fault and as a result more than a million people moved out of the state to become refugees elsewhere. The sad truth of the matter is that 'elsewhere' just doesn't exist. We have had record heat and record cold and record rainfall and record drought and record snowfall all across the country and in unthinkable places.

"All of that you likely knew through the news outlets. My job is to research and determine why. Another facet of my work has been to predict the likelihood of re-occurrence of these disasters. An impossible facet of my job has been to look into the future and see what lays in wait. In the most simple of terms, here is how it works. Let's begin with the far western states. Most of that dry land was never meant to have people living on it. Why? In addition to the San Andreas fault line, the far western states ... for all practical purposes, do not have enough sustainable water. Over the decades that demand has been met by building dams, diverting rivers and creating concrete spillways through big cities such as Phoenix. All of this ... and more ... has created its own weather system. Mother Nature doesn't like it when we tamper with the natural order of things.

"So we moved the water away from where it was put to where it was needed for large consuming communities who required it. The land which used to have water ... either above ground or below, doesn't now. Rural areas became a tinderbox for fire. Lightning storms began to set these forests ablaze and consume all the dried vegetation. Along with natural and manmade wind created by wind farms, the fires became unstoppable. Resources, wildlife, whole towns and a way of life gets destroyed with regularity in the west.

"Once the fires leave the earth barren, there is nothing left to hold back the rain that does come. So then we have either dust storms when the land is dry or mud slides when the land is wet.

"One of these dust storms was responsible for killing my four year old daughter in Tucson in 2030. The storm that ended Brenda's life had picked up a mutant strain of Hanta Virus as it was rolling along dry, barren land much like a huge tumbleweed and dropped it in an area where it entered her body. It ravaged her system ... the doctors didn't know what it was. It wasn't until several weeks later when the CDC identified the new strain being carried along the wind that the medical community sat up and begin to take notice. Brenda was one of only a few to die from the virus that year ... now there are hundreds and potentially thousands. It could become our next pandemic. In fact any number of new viruses could appear during the coming years because their once stable environment is changing quickly, and they are changing to adapt.

"While I am on the subject, lets move to northern Europe, the Arctic, northern Canada and northern Asia for just a moment. What do all these places have in common ... or did at one time? Any guesses? Permafrost. The top inches or feet of ground in areas so cold that it has stayed permanently frozen for the last thousand years ... give or take, according to location. Keep in mind that vegetation can still grow above ground and continues to contribute to the layers of earth which build up over time.

"How does permafrost hurt anything? Well it really didn't until global warming became a factor. Just an increase of a few degrees started to thaw part of these top layers and guess what happened then? For the last decade, the medical community has seen an alarming increase in a disease which wiped out untold millions of people on the Asian and European continent ... commonly known as the 'Plague' or 'Black Death'. Yes, these little virus and spores which lay dormant in the permafrost since the 1300s and 1400s have been warmed up just enough to hitch a ride on the same carriers of the middle ages ... fleas, rodents and other wild animals. If it keeps getting warmer, we will start to see diseases spring to life which are today unknown to mankind, but which killed folks during the day of Julius Caesar.

"I will get out of the Surgeon General's field and let him address these things more fully.

"Permafrost contains another danger ... carbon dioxide and methane gas. While both elements are found on earth naturally, in large quantities they can be deadly. In 1986 a lake in Africa experienced an eruption of carbon dioxide into the air above it. Being a heavy element, it stayed close to the ground, spread by the wind and as a result it displaced oxygen in the air. An entire nearby village of 2,000 people and scores of animals died from suffocation. It took some time for the scientists to figure that mystery out because it was something they had not encountered before. Imagine a landscape covered with dead bodies of people and animals with not so much as a mark on them. No sign of struggle ... water and food tested negative for poison. It took years to understand the sequence of events.

"Sigsbee Basin underwater in the Gulf Of Mexico has the highest known concentration of methane gas anywhere. Logic tells you it is at the bottom of the Gulf so it isn't a danger. Warming of the waters in the Gulf can create a restructuring of the weight of water to allow the methane to be released to the surface. In large enough quantities, a release of this methane all at once would displace all the oxygen in the air around it. Methane is also highly volatile and burns easily. Once the methane vapor reached land, a lightning strike could set off fires for hundreds or thousands of miles indiscriminately. The air would literally catch on file and burn anything and everything beneath it. Huge fireballs falling to earth would vaporize anything they touched.

"One of the biggest concerns we are now focusing on globally is the largest volcano on the planet discovered in 2013 ... called Tamu Massif at the bottom of the Pacific Ocean. The volcano, 400 miles wide and silent for 114 million years, has been sending shock waves of seismic activity for several years now. To wrap your mind around its size, imagine the distance between Atlanta and Tampa, Florida, or from Atlanta to Indianapolis, Indiana. This oceanic plateau type of volcano has a proven link with mass extinction and climate change in the distant past. I can't fathom what a full eruption would do in today's world. The tsunami alone would wipe out the western states ... and probably cover Japan. The ash falling from an eruption of this size could encircle the globe and block out sunlight to millions ... if not billions ... of people for a very long time. The Pacific Ocean would become toxic to marine life. Crop growing would cease in a huge part of the world and what would still be viable farmland would become the new 'gold standard' of modern times. One of the few things common to all humans and animals is to eat or take in enough of the sun's energy ... as with plants.

"Another great concern to scientists are the frequent small eruptions of the giant volcano lying under Yellowstone Park, called by some the biggest 'super volcano' in the world. For decades, the mud pots, geysers and boiling springs have grown in frequency and intensity to the point that the Park had to be closed to visitors ten years ago. Until now they have acted like relief valves to the caldera under Yellowstone. The question is now not 'if' but 'when' Yellowstone will erupt in convulsions not seen in this country since it has been inhabited. All of us here know the consequences of that event. Enough rock and ash would come from that eruption to bury an area around it the size of Texas. The blast alone could be more forceful that one million atomic bombs going off all at once.

"The winds carrying the rock and ash could reach 100 miles an hour and reach the east coast of this country within four days. The wind would become a caldron of hot gases. Molten rock coming out of the eruption would be 1,000 degrees ... raining down from the sky ranging in size from a house to a pea. The sulfuric acid released would go into the clouds and drop out as acid rain. I don't need to tell you how toxic that would be to anything it touched. As with an eruption of Tamu Massif, the ash would block out the sun for weeks, months or years. What would follow would be a nuclear winter. That could in itself lead to another ice age. What an irony that global warming could set off an ice age. Seismologists are following Yellowstone closely, but the truth of the matter is that except for evacuating people within a certain radius when the threat becomes imminent, nothing can be done to stop it.

"We had just a small scale glimpse of what a volcano can do when Mount St. Helens erupted in 1980.

"Along coastal Florida we are having an increasing number of waterspouts coming ashore, picking up our beaches a piece at a time and sprinkling them over nearby land masses. The beautiful beaches surrounding this entire country were built over eons from the constant ebb and flow and battering and crushing of the shells once inhabited by small invertebrates. The tourist industry which depends on these beaches of sand has been affected tremendously ... not to mention the hundreds of millions of dollars of real estate being washed away daily. While there is now a ban on new development within a mile of any beach of this country, it has become a matter of 'too little, too late'.

"Tornadoes ... I dare say everyone in this room has been impacted by them over the last few decades. While the deadly ones were fairly rare once upon a time, they now come with regularity through 'tornado alley' in the heartland of this country ... and some folks have started to call it 'tornado gully'. I don't have to go into the details of what damage these storms leave in their wake. They long ago began to devastate vast farmlands, not to mention the untold loss of life, property and food production.

"Living in Florida, I always keep one eye on my weather monitor for hurricane formation. For many decades hurricane season was officially June 1st through November 30th. The rest of the year folks could rest a little easier. NOAA has now all but eliminated those start and end dates. I have been through hurricanes in Florida during every month of the year ... even during what we call 'winter' ... December and January.

"Snowstorms and blizzards have become as unpredictable as hurricanes in recent decades. At times, they claim more lives and destroy more property than anyone ever imagined they would. A recent phenomenon has started coming with more frequency ... 'thunder snow' ... a combination blizzard, thunder, lightning, hail and sleet all in one fiercely devastating weather event. Higher drifts, higher winds, higher mortality. We also know that often a hurricane event will collide with a nor'easter which is like Mother Nature wrapping all her revenge into one big snowball and dropping it on us.

"In fact I would use that one word ... revenge ... to describe what has happened to the weather systems during the past fifty years. I see nothing to suggest these weather patterns will change. They will only intensify. Along with sweltering summer weather along the Great Lakes during January, and ice storms in Texas during July ... it has become a weather specialist's worst nightmare. The bottom line is that in this country ... and in other parts of the industrialized world ... there is no such thing anymore as 'predicting' the weather any farther out than a few days, a week at most.

"I have read and heard many people talking about 'end times' on the earth. I wouldn't pretend to be a Bible scholar, but I know the Book Of Revelation does speak of these things as 'signs'. Will any of us at this conference live to see flower gardens in the Sahara Desert, or Niagara Falls dry up, or snow shovels sold in Florida? I feel like a failure in many ways ... my whole adult life has been dedicated to learning complicated computations, statistics, studying things like ocean currents and jet streams, putting all this into a computer and having a long range weather forecast come out the other end.

"One of the most unanticipated and unpredictable factors in this equation has been the breach of the protective layer of ozone directly over this country. Everyone here knows about it whether or not you are able to acknowledge it for security reasons.

"I am sorry to say that at this point, global warming has truly become climate change in a major way. It has redrawn our maps. It has caused untold death and destruction. It has disrupted the day-to-day life of virtually everyone in this country. It has restructured the Federal Budget to the point that 'disaster relief' now consumes more of it than ever before and is starting to compete with the defense budget for top billing. Still, throwing money and manpower at these disasters has not righted this country.

"The only sure way to know what the weather will be tomorrow is to put a rock outside and the next day if it is wet, it is raining; if it is dry, the sun is out; if it is covered in white fluffy stuff, it is snowing. If the rock is gone, God help us."

As Elliott leaned back in his seat after delivering the death sentence the only sound he heard was his own breathing. 'Will somebody say something ... anything' he thought to himself as he looked around the room and saw all eyes on him.

Dr. Lazenby finally broke the silence by introducing the next speaker, the head of NOAA with whom Elliott was well acquainted. "Well Elliott I am not sure if you were trying to steal my thunder ... no pun intended ... or just shorten my speech." Everyone allowed themselves a moment of comic relief. As he continued, Elliott gazed down at his desk and became lost in his own thoughts. For the first time in all these years, he could see the whole big picture and it was all he could do to hold back tears ... both for himself and humanity. Not since Brenda died had he felt such a sense of utter despair.

After a few more speeches and adjourning for the evening meal, Elliott ate in silence. The group in the dining room sat around making polite small talk just as folks always do. Afterward everyone was invited to take a walking tour of the Camp David grounds and Elliott went along for the distraction. The smell of spring was everywhere and he took particular notice of the wildlife and vegetation as never before. He saw two Cardinals ... the red male and green female ... engrossed in their own purpose of courtship. Soon there would be a nest and eggs and new life. How blissfully unaware they are he thought.

CHAPTER 18

The following day Elliott's mood hadn't improved, but he returned to the meeting hoping to hear something which would offer some hope. The first speaker was from the head of FEMA, Dr. Katherine Hobbs. She managed that department better than it had been in decades. Her funding had been doubled in the last three years so she had the resources to mobilize people in her department and authority to deploy the National Guard during emergency situations. Death and destruction had been minimized due to her brilliant grasp of just what the Federal Emergency Management Agency could do and she used every ounce of her authority to do it. No one questioned her dedication, but the plain truth was that there were situations occurring which had no precedent. Many times she had to fly by the seat of her pants ... or skirt ... and for the most part, she had been proven up to the task.

The other speakers, doctors, members of the EPA, military and scientists from various fields of endeavor came and went with little fanfare. Elliott hoped the discussion part would be more productive than the talking. Elliott felt he had been the only one to bring something new or unknown to the conference. He had dutifully taken notes that morning and the previous afternoon in order to participate in the general discussions later that day and the following day.

After lunch was served, everyone was given an hour to refresh themselves, rest or stroll the grounds ... always under watchful eyes of guards.

When they reconvened for the discussion part of the conference, the chairs and tables had been rearranged in a circle suggesting everyone had equal standing. Dr. Lazenby opened with brief remarks of protocol.

"I want to thank each of you for attending and presenting your papers. There is no doubt in my mind ... and I doubt in yours ... that this country faces a journey into the unknown in the future. We can't undo what has been done to bring us to this point ... at least not with the speed that is required to avert a climatic catastrophe somewhere out there ... likely more than one. Feel free to speak up ... this is no time for timidity. I would ask that the person speaking confine their remarks to facts and not rhetoric or blame. Others should allow the speaker the courtesy of finishing before jumping in with a challenge or question ... which I strongly encourage. We have heard the experts tell us what the status quo is and now we need to find solutions. I will begin the discussion by outlining some of the contingency plans in place and how the Department Of Homeland Security would respond to a national disaster."

"The DHS has in place contingency plans to handle catastrophic events. We have no way of knowing the scope of what the disaster would be, but we would respond in the same way we have to others ... just enlarge our plans accordingly. One of our main concerns during any disaster is monitoring those who might take advantage of our situation. By now half the military which had once been deployed overseas is in change of defending our borders on a twenty-four hour basis. The other half is part of the DHS and it would be their responsibility to remain vigilant for internal civil disobedience and protecting infrastructure. The President would issue an executive order enacting Marshall Law throughout the fifty-four states for the duration. This task was made somewhat easier in 2037 by either admitting to statehood or granting independence to territories we previously held, so our focus can remain more centralized.

"Curfews in affected areas would be strictly enforced by either the military or National Guard. With the total ban enacted in 2036 on assault and semi-automatic weapons held by private individuals and limiting their use to military only, any individual out beyond curfew and found in possession of such weapons would be arrested and detained without bail until the national emergency has passed. The military and Guard would be instructed that if such individuals failed to respond to orders to stop for any reason, they would be subject to whatever force was necessary to detain them, including being shot. With the enactment of Marshall Law for the greater good, of course some of what we consider to be 'civil rights' would of necessity be suspended to be sorted out in the Courts once Marshall Law was lifted. For example, if a city block or the city itself is being consumed by fire and looters are scrambling with stolen property, it makes no sense to detain someone and begin by reading them their

Miranda Rights ... especially if they are armed with a weapon. Mistakes will be made, but Marshall Law gives us the teeth we need to clamp down on thugs without penalty.

"If ... or when ... the anticipated but unknown climate crisis occurs which affects millions of our population, all network and cable television in affected areas will be suspended and all broadcasting will emanate from Washington, DC. This is part of the Emergency Broadcast System tested for years, but never put in force. Local stations would be encouraged to suspend broadcast except in those areas not affected. The EBS would be a 24 hour system issuing bulletins regarding the crisis and instructions for survival. Public shelters have been designated and stocked for those who are unable to remain at home for whatever reason, but the majority of the population will be instructed to 'shelter in place'. As with any other crisis this country has faced, we expect the worst, prepare as we can, and hope for the best. None of us know how we will come out the other side of a storm until we are tested."

Other members of the panel responded to Dr. Lazenby's remarks and the discussion process had begun. It lasted the balance of the afternoon and Elliott was impressed with the civility and general sincerity each person had brought to the table ... or circle. He wavered between hope and despair ... thinking some of what he heard was just so much rhetoric and others offering positive input. Regardless, this was the only process he knew of which could get to the bottom line. Still, the basic question of how you protect a population of 400 million people from some unknown catastrophe seemed like a futile exercise.

Elliott was a pragmatist and accepted the reality that in any catastrophe there would be collateral damage ... no matter how unacceptable that concept was to the others. Most of the folks there were idealistic in their thinking to the extent that they wanted a failsafe plan to protect and save everyone. While noble in concept, it simply couldn't be done. The renegades of society would always take advantage ... would always act based on a sense of entitlement ... would always rebuke authority for self rule. He thought of Abraham Lincoln's famous quote and changed it to suit this situation ... 'you can save some of the people some of the time, but you can't save all the people all the time'.

CHAPTER 19

It was New Year's Eve in 2039 while at a friend's party that Elliott and Margaret were making the social rounds when they were approached by Joshua and Janice Adams. They knew them casually and often mingled with them at social events. They hadn't 'clicked' enough to engage them in meaningful conversation or to expand their acquaintance beyond the occasional meetings. After some small talk the Adams said they would like to become better acquainted and invited the Stewarts for mid-afternoon dinner the next day. Everyone slept in and had late breakfast on New Year's Day and a second meal later in the day ... often to the background sound of a football game.

Joshua was a primary care doctor in a large group practice (which was rare in these days ... everyone wanted a specialty) and his wife Janice was a trauma nurse at Jacksonville's largest hospital which appeared to consume her life ... both at the hospital and being on call for mass casualty emergencies. They were approaching middle age just as the Stewarts were.

After they all toasted the beginning of 2040 the group began to drift away from the party. On the short drive home they were both lost in our own thoughts. "Margaret, what do you suppose that was all about? I mean we know Joshua and Janice casually, but why would they want to pursue a friendship with us? Neither Joshua nor Janice have time for canasta parties or fund raisers. You are nearly indispensable as Business Manager at the law firm and you know my schedule works like throwing darts at a dart board."

"Let's just be pleasant and make it a nice afternoon. We know neither of them has time for charity work, so that isn't what this is about. After all, tomorrow is Friday and we can afford some social time with the free weekend coming up. I can't remember when we both had four days running without a work schedule to follow."

They went to dinner the next day ... dutifully impressed by their stunning home ... and spent a surprisingly relaxed afternoon getting to know Joshua and Janice ... or rather them getting to know the Stewarts. Margaret was thinking allowed "Odd how they always kept turning the conversation back toward us. They seemed genuinely interested in getting to know all about every detail of our lives."

"Perhaps it would be nice if we reciprocated by taking them to dinner some time next weekend ... what do you think Margaret?"

"Fine with me, but I would enjoy entertaining them in our home. Perhaps another early dinner on Sunday ... I could certainly manage that. If you agree, I will call them early in the week to find out what Janice's schedule is."

"Great."

The two couples continued entertaining each other each weekend for a month. The four were becoming good friends and learned they had a lot in common. It was the Adams' turn to host the dinner next but it turned out to be far more than just a meal.   What they discussed with the Stewarts was totally out of left field ... and downright bizarre.

CHAPTER 20... 2040

"Come in folks ... it is cold out there for February in Florida. Joshua heard on the local news that some folks in the outlying areas around Jacksonville had not only frost on the ground this morning, but saw snow flurries during the night. What about that Mr. Weatherman?"

As Elliott and Margaret made their quick entry to the house Elliott said "afraid so Janice ... and the jet stream has dropped so far down into the country, we may see more than a few flurries next week."

"Hi folks, come in and warm up by the fireplace and have a hot toddy to take the chill off ... you've got to be kidding Elliott about the snow thing next week" Joshua said as he headed to the kitchen for a refill of his drink and made two for Elliott and Margaret.

"You know Joshua, I remember when us weather forecasters would joke about it and call it the 'Siberian Express'. It occasionally got to mid-Georgia and then backed off ... repelled by the salty sea breeze and other factors."

After a little more chit chat among the four, Janice announced that dinner would be a very informal buffet and eating by the fire on folding snack tables. As agreed when they first started visiting each other for meals, the food was very casual ... nobody wanted to break a sweat on Sunday cooking all day. That day it was shrimp salad and tomato slices on hoagie rolls, cole slaw and chocolate cheesecake for dessert. Janice put her hand up in a stop gesture and said "I know Joshua, don't drag out your medical slap on the wrist about what we are having ... consider it 'food for the soul'."

They all devoured the food as though they hadn't eaten in a week ... "must be an instinct nature gives us to store up body fat when it is cold like this ... something primal ... like squirrels gathering up their nuts" Elliott remarked.

Janice started to giggle and pretty soon they were all howling in convulsive laughter.

After the laughing ran its course, Margaret said "Joshua, you and Janice know a lot about us ... what about you ... do you have any children ... and tell us lots of interesting things we don't know".

Janice began their story. "We have a grown daughter and son ... both live in Denver ... why I don't know ... said they wanted to live where there were seasons. Being so close in age and single, they rented a duplex together and have been out there about three years now ... for all Joshua and I know they seem content with no desire to come back here. Our son Alec is a doctor like his dad, except he specialized in Pharmacogenetics and Genome Therapy. Don't feel put off by that ... I had to ask Alec myself what that meant ... and he said in its most basic form, it is using cutting edge treatment tailored to an individual's once devastating disease like ALF or cancer based upon their genetic makeup. He said they were having significant success with this approach although as you might imagine the cost of administering this therapy is huge, and a lot of insurance companies don't want to cover it because it is still considered somewhat experimental.

"Our daughter Jan is a teacher, although not in the same sense of the word that any of us four can really relate to, and especially our parents. For many years now most college level classes have been taught over Skybox ... what we used to call the internet. The cost of educating younger children became so costly that the states were flooding in red ink. Something had to be done; otherwise, the entire education system would collapse for lack of funding. Congress finally took a bold step by changing the way we offer education now. The first eight years of education are still taught in group settings in schools ... for the added benefit of socializing children into society. They eliminated 'on site' teaching for all high school students except during exams when students have to actually appear at a designated facility to take the tests. Students watch the classes at home and respond to questions that come on the screen. If they don't type in an answer, the video presentation won't continue until they do. They can watch the classes as many times as needed.

"Sadly this has eliminated the additional socialization of children that age. On the plus side, it has eliminated all paper material such as books, the cost of transporting children to and from schools, and has virtually eliminated the cost of maintenance and upkeep of hundreds if not thousands of buildings once used as high schools. Some have been converted for use as libraries and government buildings or sold for public enterprise.

"Jan is very excited to have gotten into this system because, as you might imagine, teaching positions for these online classes have been reduced by about 75%. You have to be the best of the best, and the students can't help but benefit from that. What one teacher could teach in one day to maybe 150 students, one teacher can now reach thousands. She said that Colorado has been very aggressive about putting this system in place. Because Florida has a high percentage of elderly population, the actual practice of online education has just now begun development in our state.

"There has been another evolution taking shape ... colleges are now becoming specialty houses of education. All college students are required to take a specific list of general education courses during their freshman year online. They can elect to take more if they want. After that first year they are matriculated into schools which specialize in a chosen profession for the next three years of their education. We simply couldn't continue requiring four years of in house study to produce a pre-med or pre-law student and expect them to go another three or four or six more years beyond that. Some students worked half their lifetime to pay off loans, or dropped out along the way from sheer exhaustion. Anyone not going to college could spend a year at a trade school, or in the alternative spend one year in a special program of the military.

"There are still a lot of kinks to be worked out in this new way of educating people, but it is a start and over time will produce tremendous benefits to everyone. Whew ... why didn't someone stop me from droning on and on"

"My dear wife gets so involved with our Alec and Jan's lives that she gives me the same ten dollar version of what she talks to them about when really the nickle version would be just fine with me."

Margaret had listened with great interest to Janice's story and told Joshua she was fascinated by what their children were involved with. She said it was the 'dawning of a new age'.

"Margaret, it may be a new age in many ways ... certainly medicine and education are two of the areas making great progress. What Janice and I want to talk with you and Elliott about today has little to do with either ... in fact, it is a situation as old as mankind."

CHAPTER 21

"Elliott, we know a lot more about you than just what you have told us. When the University hires a Professor we on the Board Of Directors put that person under a microscope. We look for academic qualifications of course ... but another equally important factor we consider is a person's devotion ... or passion ... for his work. Just about anyone can pick up a textbook and read it aloud to a classroom of students or prepare an online lesson. You have devoted your life's work to the study of weather and climate ... publishing many papers about research findings ... taking part in any facet of the meteorological world when called upon. Elliott, I know you attended a very high profile conference in Washington last year, and I know what the conference was about. You didn't know it at the time, but your reputation preceded you and that series of meetings was built around you and what we all suspected, but only you knew for sure.

"Margaret your talents lay in organization and structure and record keeping. Being an attorney without taking the Bar exam, you were insightful enough to recognize the fact that you didn't have the competitive nature required to be a practicing attorney. Equally important, you recognized your true skills and built a career for yourself around them. I happen to know that you are considered nearly irreplaceable at the law firm you manage.

BLACK SNOW ... by Anne Rushton

"We also know about Brenda and the tragedy you suffered when she died of a mutant virus. I think that is what propelled Elliott full throttle into research. He knew first hand what global warming and weather change had caused and was determined to at least understand it ... probably knowing full well that there wasn't a thing he could do to change it ... the weather I mean."

"Janice and I have recently become a part of a very select group of people and we are asking you both to join our efforts. Some might call us 'survivalists' and while that is true, there is so much more to it. The group is led by a wealthy philanthropist ... actually a group of philanthropists located throughout the country who have recently completed survival compounds ... to be populated by people like us and you ... people who process certain survival skills and the passion to live. We don't know when a national catastrophe will hit ... we don't know what will cause it ... but we have it on good authority that the first most likely candidate would be some type of extraordinary weather event. Should that occur, there would be some warning of it ... Elliott ... you would give the 'leaders' as much advance notice as possible. After that there would be a collective notice to the participants to gather at the individual compounds for the duration of the emergency. It could be that 'it' ... whatever 'it' is ... could last for weeks, months or God forbid a year or more. Rest assured the compounds are fully functional and well stocked and perfectly designed for comfort, efficiency and most importantly, survival. We who emerge afterward could find a different life form than the one we left behind. We might or might not be able or willing to emerge ... that would remain to be seen.

"Elliott and Margaret, before I go any further or tell you more, I need to ask you to sign an 'Oath Of Secrecy' vowing to never divulge anything I have told you today ... whether you decide to join us or not. It is a matter of national security that you take and keep this vow of silence."

They sat in rapt silence and nodded, indicating they would sign, which they did.

"Now for the most important question to you both ... will you join us? I know you are in shock and your mind is a blur of confusion. You will second guess whatever decision you make for a long time. I can tell you that if you decline, we will not approach you again nor will you be allowed at the compound. If you decide to take part, everyone in the project will meet at the compound in a few weeks to meet Ben as he likes to be called, and learn about what he has put together. The message to gather will come directly from Ben to me by way of an encrypted voice mail." Elliott and Margaret stared at Joshua, then at each other. "Perhaps Jane and I will go upstairs for a few minutes to give you a chance to consider it."

After the Adams left the room, Elliott shook his head trying to unscramble his brain to grasp what he had just been told; Margaret, as usual, was contemplating the situation in a methodical way, giving weight to as many contingencies as possible. No time for a Plan B, C, D. It came down to a simple 'yes' or 'no'. "Elliott what are you thinking?"

He responded with an unmistakable catch in his voice and dewy eyes, "I don't think we have a choice Margaret ... that is if you will come with me." Margaret looked deeply into Elliott's eyes to see if she could find any doubt. When Elliott closed his eyes and looked down, Margaret grabbed his hand and said "I am all in".

The Adams came back to the room ... both the Stewarts indicated their acceptance and willingness to participate. There was no sense of excitement about the moment ... instead a somber mood which hung over them all.

CHAPTER 22

The following day Elliott and Margaret returned to work, more for the distraction it would bring than anything else. Elliott didn't immediately jump into his weatherman mode; Margaret found it nearly impossible to concentrate on her job. Each knew they had turned a corner the previous night from which there was possibly no return. Joshua told them that in a few weeks all the participants would converge in Atlanta, Georgia and from there to the compound. They would join the others, meet the leader, tour the facility, and learn what was expected of them. At that point they would be given one last chance to resign. If they committed themselves to the project, there was no turning back. Not only their lives, but the lives of the others would depend on a full participation of those selected. It truly had to be a team effort for any of them to survive.

The Stewarts had committed themselves to making two trips to Atlanta on consecutive weekends for training. They knew it would be a grueling time, traveling up and back, trying to learn as much as they could about the compound, as well as maintain their already heavy work schedules. In preparation, they had suitcases packed, ready to go on a moment's notice. It didn't take long for that moment to come. Two weeks from the weekend they committed themselves, the Stewarts received a surprise visit one evening from Joshua and Janice.

"Sorry to interrupt your evening in such an abrupt way,

but I am sure you will understand why we came unannounced."

Elliott welcomed the Adams and said "of course".

Joshua told them the first of the two weekends at the compound would be the weekend coming up. "From this point on we will not be able to communicate in any way except for personal visits. Who knows who is listening or reading voice or electronic messages. I know it sounds like we are planning some kind of malevolent act or invasion, but for the safety of everyone concerned, there can be absolutely no breach of information of what we are about to undertake." Elliott and Margaret nodded in acknowledgment.

"Here are your round trip tickets from Jacksonville to Atlanta for both weekends. Someone will be waiting to pick you up at the airport. They will meet you at the gate and will be holding a piece of torn cardboard with both your first names printed on it in red crayon. Follow him to the waiting car and from there, you will receive instructions or guidance for each step you take. Pack a suitcase as you would for any casual weekend out of town. No cameras or means of electronic communication will be allowed. Still in?" Again, Elliott and Margaret agreed and with that, Joshua and Janice departed as unceremoniously as they had arrived.

CHAPTER 23

When Elliott and Margaret arrived at Hartsfield Airport in Atlanta, they saw a gentleman at the gate holding a sign with their first names on it. Introducing himself as Ethan, he led 'Elliott and Margaret' as he called them, through the throng of people and a maze of corridors to the exit where a chauffeured limousine awaited the three. Their luggage had been collected by a lady who directed the baggage handler to the waiting car. Once fully loaded, they sped away and drove north. Being early Saturday morning with few commuters on the highway, the driver took the Interstate straight thru the city. Soon they were driving in open country ... beautiful rolling hills and lush farmlands. Elliott wondered what that bucolic landscape would look like in time to come.

He and Margaret both knew their purpose in coming so they didn't engage their greeter in conversation. Ethan broke the ice by asking the obligatory question about the flight. "Fine ... some turbulence, but nothing serious" Elliott replied.

"I know you know the reason you have been invited to come to Ben's home ... as do we all ... we are all part of the 'team' he has put together. He is hoping you will be a good fit for us ... and we for you. All your needs will be met while you are there."

Elliott and Margaret listened as they continued to watch the beautiful moving picture show from the car windows. Within an hour of landing and meeting Ethan, they had exited the interstate highway and began a fifteen minute drive on a desolate, barely maintained two lane road. They noticed a road sign as they turned in which said 'DEAD END ROAD'. During the drive they were surrounded on both sides by a thick evergreen forest. The car slowed and started to make a right turn up a slight grade in what looked like a continuation of the overgrown roadside. As the driver carefully wove his way between the trees up the slope, they could see the wooded scenery begin to part for the passage of the car.

"What the ..." Elliott stopped in mid-sentence, trying to fathom what had just happened. Margaret just stared ahead and then at Elliott. They both shivered from being part of the unknown. They quickly stared ahead and saw nothing but the same scenery as they had from the road.

Ethan assured them nothing was amiss ... they had passed through gates covered in a cloak of invisibility. The tall fence surrounding the property was also shielded from view in this manner. When the car slowed to a crawl for no reason apparent to the Stewarts, they saw what became an overhead garage door open. Elliott stammered "the house ... same thing"? Ethan nodded and they all exited the vehicle inside a garage in front of the now visible closing door.

"Let me show you to your rooms where you can rest until lunch with Mr. Jordan ... uh, Ben ... and the others." The Stewarts and Ethan left the underground garage containing various sizes and types of vehicles. They all rode an elevator which Elliott assumed was taking them to the main floor.

They worked their way through winding corridors with numerous doors ... all closed and labeled.

Ethan announced that lunch would be at noon and he would be at their door at 11:30 to show them the way. Elliott and Margaret tried to take in their suite of rooms and adjoining bathroom without moving from the spot. They knew to expect the unexpected ... but this was far beyond anything they could have imagined.

"Margaret this must be a sitting room and the room on the other side of the bath the bedroom". Elliott had taken a few steps beyond his 'parking spot'. They noticed two windows in the sitting room on the outside wall covered with shade film. "I guess another one of those 'we can see out but no one can see in' things" Elliott remarked. He supposed in due time they would be let in on this bit of image trickery.

They both looked out the windows and could see nothing but a continuous untouched forest of trees and underbrush. A few wild rabbits, some birds and a few fallen tree trunks completed the natural scene.

They decided to leave their guessing game until lunch or whenever Mr. Jordan chose to reveal his secret ... they were sure there were more. The furnishings were pleasant enough ... not luxurious but very sturdy and everything in the room obviously had a purpose. "No frills" Margaret commented ... "and just a tad institutional looking." They decided to rest during their 'free' hour before Ethan would fetch them. "Re-energize themselves" Elliott suggested, certain there was much more to come.

Ethan appeared precisely at 11:30 and assumed they were ready for his arrival. Margaret answered the door and with a wave of Ethan's hand gesturing to follow him, they were on their way to what could only be called a 'room for eating'. It was fully functional, comfortable, but no wasted space with the same semi-industrial look their suite had.

The table had seating for seventeen and with Elliott and Margaret taking their places, they acknowledged the others already assembled. Two of those seated were Joshua and Janice Adams, the doctor and nurse couple who had invited them to be a part of this group. There were three empty seats and precisely at the noon hour Benedict Jordan entered the room and took his place at the head of the large oval table. Immediately a large horizontal partition in the east wall opened, a stainless steel bar slid forward on which contained a sumptuous meal. 'Ben' as he asked to be called announced that food service was buffet style and a line would form beginning with the person to his left and go around the table. "Enjoy your meal as soon as you have returned to the table" he announced and with that, the line began to form.

When everyone had returned to the table, Elliott and Margaret noticed the two remaining seats had been taken at some point during the self service ... the two empty chairs to Ben's right. The meal tasted as good as it looked and was more than adequate in variety and quantity with little leftover.

BLACK SNOW ... by Anne Rushton

After they had finished eating, Ben asked the assembled group to follow him to the gathering room after they had returned their place settings to the bar ... plates in a stack, glasses in the rack, napkins in the basket and utensils in the aluminum container.

Elliott leaned over to Margaret and whispered "rather like a military environment wouldn't you say?" Margaret let her guard down just enough to exhale and smile.

CHAPTER 24

When everyone was gathered and took one of the seats in the gathering room, Ben heartily welcomed everyone and said "I don't need to tell you why you are here ... for many of you, this is the first time you have met anyone in this group; a few others know each other."

"As you know when you were asked ... and agreed ... to become part of this group, you have been sworn to secrecy for your own safety and every else's in this room to never speak to anyone outside the group about things you already know and things you will learn this afternoon and tomorrow before you depart as stealthily as you arrived ... each returning to their normal day-to-day lives.

"Each person in this group was hand picked ... either by me or someone already hand picked by me. You were chosen because of your profession, and also because you met other stringent requirements you were first asked about during your initial contact. You didn't fill out any forms, but some of what I am about to tell you may remind you of conversations I or someone in this group had with you.

"Everyone here has basic survival skills with proven experience thru Scouting, being a naturalist, a camper, a former Prisoner Of War, a former military enlistee who fought in combat, or someone with martial arts training and experience.

"You are here because you have a certain level of proficiency in the use of weapons and have indicated you had no fear or hesitation to use them should a situation warrant it.

"All of you are leaders in your profession, but not what I would call 'famous'. This group has no place for an ego or arrogance or an 'attitude'. You are mature enough to be of use to yourself and others, but not so much that age related issues would be a handicap. You might modestly think of yourselves as on 'top of your game'. Modest self confidence is a prized attribute for anyone to have.

"None of you hold a particular political party affiliation. You must be an independent thinker ... flexible and eager to 'think outside of the box' during problem solving.

"No one here ... including myself ... now has or ever had an addiction to tobacco, alcohol, food, any type of illicit drug, a criminal history, has an ongoing medical condition or bad habit. Incidently, loving Brownies is not considered an addiction; otherwise, I couldn't be part of this group.

Everyone responded with a laugh and it softened the tone of an otherwise very serious speech.

"All of you here have exhibited a strong sense of self, yet are compassionate, trustworthy and willing to work for good of the common cause.

"None of you have obligations of support to other people ... either you are single, childless or your children now live on their own. None of you have living parents. Of course you all have friends and a network of colleagues at your work, but you have indicated a willingness to be able to step away from that network if your life depended on it.

"You might be wondering how I know these things to be true about each of you. Trust me, there are ways of learning about people you don't even want to know about.

"You might also be wondering just about now who I am because you were told nothing about me during your quote unquote 'interviews' ... and yes there were more than one. You were personally screened, discreetly observed on more than one occasion, and engaged in casual conversations by complete strangers.

"First I will tell you who you are and then I will tell you who I am. Please stand, put the name tag on that you were given prior to lunch and be recognized as I call your first name ... as you will always be called ... no room here for any last names and certainly you need no titles or degree letters after your name. By the way, I took a page out of Michael Eisner's book for this process. You may recall that many years ago when Walt Disney World was built in Florida and he was the head of operations there, he used this same process. He walked everywhere with the name tag that said simply his first name 'Michael', as did every other person working there. Brilliant idea don't you think ... wish it had been mine."

CHAPTER 25

Ben began to introduce everyone. "Joshua is a doctor. He brings many years of formal education and experience as a primary care physician to the table. If needed, he can dispense medications from our pharmacy, perform dentistry and limited surgery.

"Janice is Joshua's wife. She has been a trauma nurse at a metropolitan area's largest hospital for many years. She works rotating shift duty, meaning she is able to adjust her biological clock as the need arises. She is and has been for years also 'on call' for mass casualty emergencies.

"Ethan is an architect ... the architect who designed and built this place to my specifications and should the need arise, would assume the maintenance of all systems here. Incidently, we will refer to this building as the 'house' and the entire property as the 'compound'.

"Winston is a hydrologist ... a water specialist. He has worked and consulted on some of the biggest water resource problems in the country. In the never ending effort to take water where it is plentiful and somehow get it to places that have very little, Winston has pioneered a number of uh ... shall we say 'ground breaking' projects. Pun intended. You will learn just how important his work is when we tour the building in detail tomorrow morning.

"Genevieve ... pronounced 'Jon-ve-ev' is a renowned chef of many disciplines. She started working in the fast food industry, later was educated at one of the finest culinary institutes in this country and since then has worked in various capacities in fine dining establishments and hospital kitchens. She is also a dietary specialist and nutritionist. In other words, she knows the proper and best fuel to put into our bodies to get the best out of them. I hear a couple of stifled laughs because of the way I put that ... let me rephrase and say to provide our bodies with the best fuel and leave it at that. Feel free to laugh aloud at any time ... a good belly laugh is food for the soul and a great tension release ... wouldn't you agree Genevieve?" She laughed in spite of herself.

"Fawn is the one and only kitchen assistant to our chef. She, too, has proven her mettle in the kitchens of fine dining establishments ... and followed Genevieve into working in hospital kitchens. She made that her life's career and is now the head nutritionist at a medium sized hospital in Virginia. Don't let her gentle name fool you into thinking she isn't a strict taskmaster because she is. Fawn and Genevieve will be the two we depend on to keep us alive.

"Claudia has been the director of housekeeping at one of Atlanta's biggest hotels for virtually her entire adult life. By way of continuing education, she understands the term 'germ warfare' better than likely anyone else at this gathering. It has been her responsibility to oversee all the cleaning maintenance of what needs to be a sterile environment ... or keep it as close to that as she can.

"Jo and Amber are Claudia's had picked assistants in housekeeping. Their work ethic is beyond question and their dedication to their life's career is above reproach. None of the three have ever been cited for a discipline measure.

"Drake is one of our three security specialists. He is a retired Marine, having spent twenty years in the service of this country. He is big in stature and keeps himself in perfect physical condition. His medals for honor, bravery, use of weaponry, duty, going above and beyond service would weigh his jacket down so much it would be a burden for any of us to even wear. Part of his security duty includes driving the car which picked many of you up at the airport, and the other vehicles here ... some of which you saw as you entered the garage.

"Leah is part of our security team. She and Drake have been married for 20 years. They devoted themselves to service by sacrificing parenthood. She was also a career Marine and received enough medals and ribbons to rival Drake's any day. She also earned two Purple Hearts. These two are fearless and exemplary as their military records would attest to. You may remember Leah being in the passenger seat of the car you came in either yesterday evening or this morning.

"Jamison is the third part of our security team. As a retired member of the Navy Seals, not much else needs to be said ... or can be said ... about his background or credentials. Don't let his lean stature fool you. He has used it to his advantage on many assignments where a larger person couldn't slide through a tunnel or swim under water unnoticed. He is a widower and his daughter is living in London where she is pursuing a doctorate degree in genetic engineering.

"Elliott is a meteorologist and climatologist at a large coastal University. In addition to his work as Professor of these two related fields, he works with NOAA during hurricane season ... which until recent years was a six month period ... now it is more like year round due to climate change. He has not only education, experience, but his passion for his work has led to years of research. He has had many articles published in the academic journals. To his advantage, Elliott is the sort of person who could go unnoticed in a crowd. Mr. Clean Cut, quiet average looking American. Once among his peers in his own milieu, he most definitely has a commanding presence. Regardless of height everyone in the room looks up to him. In addition to having control of our tech room, he will also serve as our communications specialist.

Margaret held her breathe as Elliott's qualifications and responsibilities were described, wondering what value she could bring to the table. An attorney can't do much without clients, cases and access to the Courts.

"Margaret will be our organization specialist, keeper of records and historian. She is General Manager of a large law firm in a big city. Including all the support staff, she oversees and coordinates the work of thirty people. She herself is an attorney, but not practicing since she elected some time ago to not sit for the State Bar Exam. Her organizational and record keeping skills will be invaluable to us as our Organizational Specialist, Record Keeper and Historian. She will also maintain a daily calendar and keep track of what day and date it is. Don't laugh ... living in a cloistered environment can play havoc on a person's psyche and without our daily routines to follow, one can become lost to the progression of time. Her structure and routine is very unforgiving and she is proficient in the use of all modern office electronics. She will know where every one of you are and what you are doing at any given time of day. I suppose years ago Margaret you would have been called 'Geek In Charge'. Margaret and Elliott have also been married for 20 years.

As she sat back down, Margaret realized that Ben actually knew her better than she knew herself. Indeed, she had kept meticulous organizational status records of cases, Court appearances, vacation schedules. Part of her work included researching precedent cases, coordinating teleconferences on Skype, and seeing to it that everyone was where they should be at any given time. The bottom line was she was the cog in the wheel around which all the spokes revolved and was the 'go-to' person for problem solving.

"We all need a spiritual advisor regardless of who or what our God is, and we have a fine one in Samuel. He is a retired military Chaplain. Samuel brings a vast experience with him of guiding, counseling, encouragement to all groups of faith ... and also to those who do not profess a faith. Before he joined the military Samuel was a board certified psychologist for several years, and I can't think of a better combination of skills. He will help us over the rough spots ... and you can count on their being those times. We, after all, will be a small boat in a vast ocean of turmoil. Sadly, Samuel lost his wife two years ago to long standing medical issues.

"Polly rounds out our group. She has been my personal barber and groomsman for many years. She will see to it that we all stay well trimmed and groomed. While we don't have a plan in place called 'the end game', at some point we might return to our old ways of life. When we emerge from our shelter we don't want to look like ancient cavemen. Her department will be well stocked with everything she needs to keep us looking and feeling human. She volunteered to give each one of us a deep tissue massage once a week if and when we are gathered here 'for the duration'. Something to look forward to ... which is in reality why we are here ... on a grand scale.

"While not planned that way, we have nearly an equal gender division represented here, and as archaic as it now sounds, we have a diverse group of ethnic backgrounds. My number one criteria in selecting you was based only on character, experience, reliability and willingness to participate. Another consideration I took into account was your location ... all within a three hour drive.

"That introduces everyone and we will have a thirty minute break to refresh ourselves with beverage and snacks. Please don't wander off from this room ... mingle and talk among yourselves. Before we break, you will be given new badges to wear which identifies you by first name and the role you will play here, if needed. Feel free to discuss any part of what I have just told you about."

CHAPTER 26

Everyone partook of the refreshments which Genevieve and Fawn had silently presented on a rolling cart. Some wondered around the room, some looked out the film shaded windows, considering what they were committing themselves to. Some chatted. All were anxious to return to their seat and hear Ben talk about Ben.

"Who am I? In actual truth, I am a wealthy man and a humanitarian. I have made it my life's work to use the vast inheritance I received to try and help move society along in a better direction whenever I could. I have a foundation headed by loyal, skilled people who examine grant applications for endowment. Outside of that situation, I have made it my goal to perform random acts of kindness as many times and to as many folks as I could. I find it hard to sleep at night if I haven't sought out that opportunity each day.

"I am Benjamin Jordan and I lived in Texas most of my young life. I live here now. I came from wonderful, wealthy parents who did not shower me with the material side of life. I didn't know I was any different from my friends. My parents and three siblings lived within the means of those in our neighborhood in Austin. We didn't look any different. Not until I was out of high school did my father reveal to me the vast fortune he had built from the small fortune he inherited when Grandpa died. Grandpa made his fortune by being on the cutting edge of high tech developments in Houston during what became known as the 'Space Age' back then. Grandpa died before I was old enough to know him and I will forever be sad about that. I was taught a strong work ethic by my parents and because we were so gifted financially, I should spend my life 'giving back' while pursuing my own interests, whatever they may be.

"I am now 60 and have turned over the philanthropy part of my life to a foundation run by very trusted friends and a few relatives. I make an appearance occasionally at the foundation just to let them know I still have my finger in the pot and on the button. My wife of 35 years died five years ago and I decided then that I would do what I had dreamed of doing for several years ... doing everything I could to perpetuate the human race in the event of catastrophe. I'm not part of one of these 'survivalists' who builds a shelter in the desert and arming myself with canned corn and assault rifles ... although we have both corn and rifles here.

"My desire went beyond just saving my own behind. I wanted to create a place for a group of specialists to live through and who could live beyond whatever disaster occurred and come out the other side of it. If this country was so mutilated by whatever happened that starting over was an unlikely event then ... well, I haven't planned that far ahead because I have confidence in myself and this group ... and many other groups like us ... to create some foundation to build on.

"Yes, there are other groups and places very similar to this one ... perhaps a dozen or twenty by now ... in this country and mostly near the eastern seaboard who have put together a plan based on the model we created. By 'we' I mean me and friends of mine who are also well endowed financially, who have like minds. I include in that group my architect who developed the structure you now find yourselves in. He gathered other architects and they collaborated for nearly a year before the first shovel of dirt was ever turned. Each of us 'leaders' for lack of a better word gave our project a name ... this one I called 'Jardin' ... not to sound like my last name, but a Spanish word for 'garden' ... where all things are planted, grow, bloom and come to fruition for the sole purpose of producing another generation. People, cows, lilies of the field, butterflies, snakes, gnats, fish, armadillos ... that is our sole purpose during the journey and to keep the journey going.

"My three grown children, their spouses and children are all part of another compound like this ... one whose special focus is on family groups.

"OK, so we know about each other now, we know why we are here and why we might need to return for an extended stay. What do you think the catalyst was for this whole idea taking root in my mind?

Margaret spoke without thinking ... "Haboobs and wind farms".

"True on both counts Margaret, but it is what is behind the Haboobs and what the wind farms created that was part of the motivation. You see, it is sadly left to the folks with free time ... for the most part those of us who already have enough to live on ... to really devote ourselves to serious thinking and research matters other people just fight or legislate against. We can use our gifts of time and money selfishly for ourselves or as I have tried to do, use my gifts to include others ... what would be the greater good for mankind.

"Most of you remember hearing the name Bill Gates from the early years of this century. He did just that. At one point he was the richest man in the world. As he matured, he came to understand that wealth brought with it responsibility. Another of the richest men in the world a few decades older than Bill, Warren Buffet, liked what he saw Bill and his wife doing. At some point they pooled most of their considerable resources ... money ... to create an enormous money pot from which to dip. To use the wealth in a good and prudent way to help the most people. In the intervening years, the Gates Foundation has provided immeasurable good to untold millions of people. I think you would find something in the Bible about 'from whom much is given, much is expected'. That sums up the premise under which I and the other 'leaders' operate, although it isn't necessarily because we feel compelled by spiritual beliefs. It is a debt we feel we owe.

"So now you have some idea of my philosophy ... and here is why I focused part of my wealth on 'Jardin'. During the gift of free time, I began to think on a higher level than

107

just day-to-day about events. I started to see a trend in real climate change. During the early 21st century, Vice President and Presidential Candidate Al Gore took on the issue of climate change ... he made it his personal challenge. People laughed. Congress was too busy fighting wars, arguing and spending money on other useless things. I knew a lot about Al Gore and knew how sincere he was. I called him one day several years ago and asked if he would consult with me. I sent my plane for him and we met for several days in the suite of rooms I had reserved for him at a hotel in Austin.

"What I heard from him nearly knocked my boots off ... you know us Texans, we have to wear boots to fit in anywhere whether it's a saloon or a board room. Anyway, I had read his book several times and began to do my own research. Based on the foundation Al laid for me and what I learned on my own convinced me that America was in peril ... not from an invader across any border or across any ocean ... but from what was directly overhead.

"For many years scientists had known there was a hole in the ozone layer at the 'bottom' of the earth and had speculated how it happened and when and what the consequences would be. What they didn't know until just a few years ago ... and kept to themselves ... was that there was another hole directly over the United States. Why? Being the most industrialized country on the planet, we had burned the hole ourselves with toxic emissions relentlessly for two hundred years.

BLACK SNOW ... by Anne Rushton

"When I think back on it, it was laughable that Presidents and Governors mandated that vehicles would have to increase their 'miles per gallon' by two or three or five miles within the next decade. It was already too late for that pitiful lip service. What needed to be said was, *'folks we have screwed ourselves and by golly the climate change is already on us. Quit thinking about how to make the next mortgage payment to keep up with the neighbors and go dig yourself a hole to live in. We are all damn near toast'*. The powers that be couldn't afford to say that by then ... mass panic would set in, the stock market would crash, banks would close, goods and services would be in chaos, food wouldn't be easily available and the entire country would erupt into a mass riot. Like it or not, those 'powers' had to stay the course and just keep on keepin on with the charade.

"It isn't a question of 'if' but 'when' this country in particular will undergo such a radical change in weather that it will become a land of 'survival of the fittest'. That, my friends and colleagues is why you are here. You have agreed to help yourself ... and humanity to succeed beyond whichever catastrophic event will be virtually unsurvivable without extreme preparation. The problem has gone far beyond 'weather change' and has become 'climate change' knocking on the front door. At some point it will cease knocking and take the door out with one fell swoop. Nothing behind the door will have a chance of survival ... except for MAYBE us and like minded folks in the other compounds.

"Enough for now ... I am sure I have scared the daylights out of some of you ... one in particular I have not and that is Elliott, our meteorologist and climatologist. Am I correct Elliott?"

"Yes Ben, sadly I concur with your findings, hypotheses and probable case scenarios. It's just a matter of which comes first."

With that Ben ended his speech and invited everyone to freshen up and arrive for dinner at 6:00 P.M.

CHAPTER 27

Elliott and Margaret laid on their bed just to relax from their time in the chairs and slow their mind from the processing. For a long time they didn't say anything.

"Well Elliott it would seem to me you have certainly been keeping a tight lid on your work for a very long time."

"Margaret, I really haven't been convinced of my own findings until Ben's speech. I could have given it word-for-word myself. You know I can't discuss my meeting at FEMA, but it was along these same lines. Until now I have been so absorbed in the bits and pieces that I had nearly failed to see the big picture. Besides, you had the wind knocked out of you when Brenda died and I couldn't bring myself to talk to you about 'maybe this will happen' sometime in the future."

"During the hours we have been here at Jardin our way of thinking and way of life has shifted at least ninety degrees. We know more about our future than I ever wanted to know. It's like looking into a dark crystal ball and seeing nothing but dark fog hovering over devastation. What do you think it will be Elliott?"

"Neither I nor Ben nor any of the others ... here or at the other compounds ... have that crystal ball you mentioned. It could be any of the above or something we hadn't even considered like nuclear fallout from war. The middle east has been such a hotbed of smoldering tension for so long now ... decades really ... that any of them could push that button now.

"That's why President Nelson issued the executive order she did on the day after her inauguration in 2027. That we were tired of war ... exhausted from it as participants ... depleted from it financially ... exhausted from it as bystanders and observers ... despondent from it emotionally and spiritually and ethically ... that from that day forward America was pulling back its involvement with any other country's strife, riots, struggles or civil war. There was still room for humanitarian efforts and assistance, but there would be nothing for weapons, boots on the ground or missiles in the sky.

"She said almost all of the resources in this country would be directed inward ... to take care of our own problems ... rebuild aging and collapsing infrastructure ... get a real handle on the crumbling health care system ... restructure and eliminate budget waste as never before with the line item veto power she had ... things that had been neglected for decades to serve the common good were going to get fixed one way or another. Period.

"She knew that the war mongers and military would be the first to voice displeasure with this. She assured that group that all active and current American Embassies would remain intact for the safety of our citizens who traveled abroad, and she had a plan for maintaining a full military structure, at the ready, at all times. Half of them would be used to bolster the growing Department Of Homeland Security, including funds for research and development of super sensitive international surveillance. The identification and monitoring of terrorist groups would be perfected to the point of totally eliminating them being one step ahead of us on any occasion. Her plans for the remaining group was to construct military bases around our entire border which would be fully staffed, trained and ready to defend this country from intrusion or invasion by land, sea or air."

"Her second executive order ... issued a week later to give the population time to digest the implications of her first order ... was to ban lobbyists from Congress effective the next day ... that the members of Congress who were elected by their constituency would return to the pioneer days mentality, which is to say they would serve the people who elected them and no one else. As a punitive measure, individuals in Congress would be immediately dismissed from office if found to be cavorting with a lobbyist either on the table or under it, and be subjected to public ridicule and shame and the forfeiture of all of their future Congressional benefits.

"The people were so empowered by her bold actions, her clear understanding of what Americans wanted, they even successfully petitioned to call a new Constitutional Convention whose sole purpose was to Amend the Constitution to set new term limits for Congress. The successful outcome of that convention put ballots in every state election to do the same. For the first time since the era of Washington, Adams and Jefferson we no longer had career office holders. Of course some say we 'threw out the baby with the bath water' by eliminating the very good office holders when they were just hitting their stride, but overall it worked toward the common good of all. Many of the States followed suit with term limits and eliminated post-service benefits of office holders.

"I tell you Margaret, the things she did during her first year in office were unbelievable ... it took a woman with balls to stand up and truly speak for what they used to call the 98%. We could almost hear a collective sound of people falling to their knees in thanksgiving. The surprising thing is, very few career politicians challenged her. They knew they weren't playing in the 'good old boys club' anymore, and that American history was about to be rewritten.

"The truly sad part of it is that while she has managed to get this country back on its collective feet during those eight years using common sense and pandering to no one, the country is now on crutches without even knowing it. The damage has been done and I don't think anything can be done now to turn it around. Mother Nature seems to have a self destruct button that keeps getting pushed."

"So which grim reaper will get us first Elliott?"

"Without wearing a blindfold and just throwing darts at a dart board, my best educated and researched guess would be snow."

"Snow? You mean the stuff kids love because they get out of school ... and make snow angels in ... and build snowmen from ... and eat ... and bring in as snowballs for the freezer so they can have snowball fights in July ... THAT snow?"

"Well Margaret, snow and hurricanes combined actually."

"Have you really lost your mind Elliott? Snow comes in winter in the north; hurricanes come in summer down south."

They both had been laying on their back staring at the ceiling during this conversation of doom. Elliott turned onto his side and looked at Margaret directly as she turned her face toward him revealing tear stained cheeks. "Margaret, remember Sandy? The hurricane that made its way up the coast with near tornadic winds ... and was so huge the destruction reached several hundred miles inland ... and left snow in the mountains of West Virginia in 2012? I think that was just a practice run."

Margaret froze and they just stared at each other for what seemed minutes. She was finally starting to wrap her head around what could happen ... on a massive scale ... if the conditions were just so ... if everything came together at just the right ... or wrong time ... an apocalyptic weather event caused by climate change which would paralyze hundreds of thousands if not millions or even tens of millions of people ... and for how long.

"Am I the last of the group to know Elliott?"

"Ben and the leaders of all the other compounds know. Ben's architect, Ethan of course and Winston who designed the water systems. Joshua and Janice ... it took some real persuasion for them to join and leave their life's work behind. They both felt ethically bound to their medical professions, but in the end could see the big picture. As you know, they both retired last year and now do volunteer work, visiting their two grown children in Colorado and biding their time.

"I know of course, and now you. The President, Vice-President, the Presidential Cabinet, the head of the National Guard as well as the Joint Chiefs Of Staff, NOAA, DHS and FEMA know. Tonight after dinner Ben will distribute study sheets to the rest about what we have just discussed. By the way, everyone here ... and in the other compounds, will be issued 'Diplomatic Immunity' for any acts they might be required to take during a national emergency after they sign an 'Oath Of Allegiance' tomorrow before leaving. In a sense we will become diplomats from our own country to our own country."

"You mean like if we have to shoot someone?"

"Margaret, you could do it if it meant saving the compound or your life. None of us need the additional burden of worrying about the 'legal' consequences of our actions."

"Do you and the others 'in the know' ... meaning meteorologists ... have any idea when this could happen ... in terms of days, months, weeks, years from now?"

BLACK SNOW ... by Anne Rushton

"Let's talk some more later."

They made their way back thru the maze of corridors and arrived for dinner at 5:45 P.M. As they took their same seats, they looked at the other faces at the table trying to get a readout of their thoughts and emotions. Not one would divulge their feelings by look or gesture.

Ben's appearance and seating was the signal for forming a buffet line once again. He announced after everyone was reseated that he had planned some diversion for everyone tonight. A state of the art gym was available for exercise or taking a walk around the natural setting outside. Elliott and Margaret decided to watch old movies in their suite ... something silly or slapstick or historical. Anything to change the atmosphere. The gathering room also served as a library stocked floor to ceiling with movies, books, games, cards ... anything one could want for a diversion.

At the end of the meal Ben said that after they retired to their rooms for the night, they would have access on their electronic center to information somewhat like a 'FAQ', although these really were not 'answers' to 'frequently asked questions' since this was a new journey for everyone at every table at every compound. More like 'answers to questions you might have come up with since this whole concept was first revealed to them'.

"Breakfast will be served at 8:00 A.M. after which we will have a walking tour of the entire compound. By the way, in the morning before the tour we will ask you to electronically

117

sign an 'Oath Of Allegiance' which will be explained in the data sheet I just mentioned. If ANYONE feels that they ... for whatever reason ... cannot be depended on to become part of this group in the event of a real emergency, please let it be known by raising your hand now.

"OK ... I see no hands which means I haven't scared you away. You also understand the importance and need for a compound like we have here for the 'just in case', although I have to tell you that I have it on very good authority that there is a high probability that 'just in case' really means 'it's a matter of when and not if'. Good ... still no hands showing.

"As you were told on your ride here, you can't take anything away from the compound with you that would identify your association with it, or its existence. Relax tonight ... if you can ... try to bring yourself to fully embrace the concept that you are doing something needed ... not just saving your own life ... but maybe, just maybe the project will serve a just and noble purpose for the greater good."

When they returned to their room Elliott asked Margaret what she would like to see on what was once called a television. Now it was the 'electronic center' ... or EC ... which controlled a computerized television, disk player, radio, telephone, Skype viewer and virtually every feature in the room ... lighting, heating, humidity, air conditioning, the compound intercom, individual water heaters in each bath; even the mattresses were controlled electronically to conform to an individual's sleep outline ... giving the sensation of being weightless.

"I suppose we should read Ben's data sheet on the EC first, and if we still have the energy for it, maybe some old nonsense western where the cowboy gets the girl."

"You sound a little sarcastic Margaret ... or are you just having a case of sensory overload?"

"Probably both. Sometimes sarcasm can be a cover for fear. Talking to you over recent years about climate problems, I have become convinced that civilization is all but doomed. Elliott, the thought has occurred to me that if I save myself and do whatever I can to help save the others here, do I really want to return to whatever part of life is left on the outside?"

"I think we have all had that same thought ... or doubt ... and this is one time that we each have to answer that question for ourselves. There really isn't room in this group for someone unwilling to put their whole heart into the project ... whatever the outcome. For myself, I feel like I have been given an opportunity to make a difference and I don't want to lose the chance of saving myself in the process."

"OK ... let's see what Ben has to say."

CHAPTER 28

"If you are watching this, it means you are one of the select few with skills, courage, knowledge, commitment and determination to take on this challenge. I commend you for making it this far. Just agreeing to come here was a big step.

"Today we learned about each other and tomorrow you will learn about the compound I have put together. Feel free to ask questions or make comments as we go along the tour. I would love to think that Ethan and I have covered most of the bases, but I am sure there is room for improvement ... or some idea we haven't even considered.

"How is this entire project of perhaps up to 20 compounds funded? Along with the outline of investors I told you about today, we have some government funding. Not for the physical property or compound ... before the government would even consider including us in their budget, the collective 'we' investors had to prove ourselves. We had to design, obtain suitable property and build the actual compound. Once we made that personal investment, the government funded all our furnishings and supplies to sustain each compound for a period of two years. Don't bother looking in the Congressional Record for anything related to the compound project ... it isn't there. It is part of the 'Black Budget' known only to those on a 'need to know' basis.

"While I am on the topic, when you get back to your home, don't bother trying to find us on the Skybox ... or internet as it used to be called. We don't exist.

BLACK SNOW ... by Anne Rushton

"Will all your needs be met at the compound? You are probably also wondering, but too polite to add 'free of charge'. Your talent and willingness to participate is the currency you will need to bring with you, along with your personal treasured possessions. No doubt you have noticed your rooms are spartan. There is a reason for that. We want each of you to have your own special items here ... feel free to bring as much as you want ... within reason ... to make your quarters feel like a home away from home.

"What means will be used to determine when we need to put the compound into full operation? Elliott and I will make that final decision. We fully expect that the need for the compound will be weather related and who better than our own Professor of Meteorology and Climatology to know when it is the 'real deal'. In fact that will be our password ... 'the real deal'.

"How will you get here when the real deal happens? You will be notified by either Ethan or I by the password that the time has come to assemble. Drive your own car ... or if you are part of a couple, come together in one vehicle. There is a separate empty, climate controlled underground bunker in which to store your vehicle. I think all of you own at least one vehicle powered by hydrogen or electric fuel cells. That 'fuel' will be available and plentiful for use at the compound and your vehicles once you leave.

"As we tour feel free to ask questions or open a discussion about any part of the compound. Nothing is 'off

limits' to anyone in our group ... for we must think of ourselves like that ... a group. The old saying, 'one for all and all for one' couldn't be more appropriately applied than to us. We will meet in the gathering room after breakfast.

"We won't have time tomorrow to go through all the fine details of everyone's responsibility and give you a chance to familiarize yourself with your work room, so I am asking that you return next weekend for that. On Saturday you will need to learn what every button is for and how to use it. On Sunday we will have somewhat of a dress rehearsal ... actually go through the day, each of you bringing your abilities to life as though you were living here."

CHAPTER 29

The following morning, everyone served themselves and ate without conversation. They were all anxious to get a look at the compound and see how it had been built for survival. Ben brought out his electronic signing DPad ... 'document pad' ... and asked if everyone felt comfortable signing the 'Oath Of Allegiance' referred to in his statement which he assumed everyone had viewed on the EC the previous night. "Anyone here want to back out now?" Seeing no hands raised, Ben passed the DPad around and everyone signed it.

Ben reminded them that by signing the document they were swearing to an oath of allegiance to him, to themselves, and to all the others to not discuss any aspect of the project with anyone now or ever. "The consequence of such a slip of the tongue would result in being barred from the project. The government and everyone else would disavow any knowledge of what you talked about ... and would deny having had any contact with you. In other words, you would be made to look like a fool and be left out to dry ... or freeze ... or whatever catastrophe brings the group together. I can't stress this enough ... there are no second chances. Understood?" To which everyone nodded in agreement.

As each person entered the gathering room, they were drawn to the center oblong table covered with what appeared to be blueprints spread out. Yesterday the table was against the wall adjoining the dining room and adjacent kitchen and was used for refreshment service. The chairs they sat in had formed a circle in the center. Today the table was the main focal point and chairs had been pushed back to the opposite wall.

For ease in understanding, these architectural prints did not contain technical designs of water, sewer, electrical or structural systems. Only the front and rear views of the main building, and the underground bunker for their vehicles were shown. There were also renderings of each floor's layout. They noticed the house contained three floors, the one they were on being the top. The top two floors of the building had been built with a convex front of glass ... or some synthetic ... facing south and the back wall was straight across ... somewhat like a pie that had been sliced in two.

The top two levels were built in the 'half pie' configuration while the bottom level was square and fully underground. The graphics were easy to understand and very precise. Someone pointed out that the floor they were on had the large dining room and kitchen in the front ... facing south ... and the large oblong gathering room was in the center adjacent to the dining room. The other three sides of the gathering room were straight and shared a common wall with a row of smaller rooms on all sides beyond the gathering room. A hallway separated these small rooms from yet another set of rooms ... each one sharing a common wall with the next. These rooms were on the outside wall of the compound, so as to provide windows for the occupants.

The floor below them was divided into two areas. The room on the west was a storage room for linens and food; the room on the east contained a gym and recreation facilities. As with the top floor these two areas faced south with a convex glass wall separating the areas from the outside.

The underground floor or basement was likewise divided into two sections. The west area was labeled 'operating systems' and the east area 'compound vehicles and weapons'. A footnote stated that only Ben and the security personnel had access to the area containing the vehicles and weapons by way of the east elevator near the dining room. Another footnote indicated that the operating systems area could only be accessed by Ben, Ethan and Winston by way of the elevator on the west. A third footnote indicated that the storage area could only be accessed by the housekeeping and cooking staff using the west elevator. All done by fingerprint recognition. There was a small room to the west of the kitchen which contained what appeared to be an elevator; the same configuration was drawn into the plans for the floor beneath them as well we the basement.

Ben appeared about twenty minutes after everyone else had entered the gathering room and asked if they had had enough time to study the 'house plans'. If so, he would ask them to take a seat so he could give some brief overall description of the workings of the compound.

"The compound itself is located on four acres square ... not four square acres ... but four acres north to south by four acres east to west ... a total of sixteen square acres. The compound you are in now sits in the exact center of that land. The land is covered entirely with evergreen trees of many varieties ... some which grow very tall and all the way down to the ones which spread along the ground. The reason for this is obvious ... it provides a perfect cover for any outside activity one of us might have to undertake. Generally speaking, once you enter this fortress for the 'real deal' you won't need ... or want ... to go back out."

With a flick of a switch, the room darkened and the blueprints appeared on the floor in front of the chairs. Pointing to the blueprints he said "the exterior of everything you see on those drawings is covered with a cloak of invisibility. This cloak was actually developed by the military during the 2020s after many years of experiment for use on the battlefield. It was our good fortune we were allowed to use it in all our compounds. In a sense, this is a battlefield and the enemy will be some type of natural disaster. The simple concept of the cloak is to hide whatever it is in front of. The eight feet tall chain link fence surrounding the property is covered with the cloak inside and out. The house is covered completely on the outside and roof. We can see out but no one can see in ... in fact, the house disappears to an outsider as all of you noticed on your drive up here when you arrived. If anyone uninvited was to breach our sophisticated security system unnoticed and be so unfortunate to accidently come in contact with one of the exterior walls, they would get quite a jolt ... not only from electricity which is low enough so as not to kill or injure the wildlife ... but the psychological damage of that experience would be sufficient to render the individual senseless for life. Don't concern yourselves, someone actually getting to the house by accident is extremely remote."

As Ben continued, he highlighted each area with a laser pen. "The convex front looks like glass, but it is a special material called LAMEX which is an acronym for a very long name and it can be made in any size ... for small scale use by law enforcement agencies and others who need special shielding ... or on a large scale. It can be made flexible enough to wear as clothing or strong enough to support the roof of a building as it does here ... along with the steel girders and pilings. The secondary use for the synthetic glass covering the southern exposure on the top two floors is to draw the sun rays into special collection units built into the first three feet of flooring on each level. Even during a blizzard on earth, the sun is still emitting the same volume of rays it always does. Engineers know how to capture that wasted energy and either use it or store it in fuel storage cells for future use.

"Yesterday you spent time in the dining room, saw the adjacent kitchen and we met for discussion here in the gathering room. The three walls of this room are adjacent to a set of rooms which are your individual work rooms. Directly across from these rooms, and separated by one continuous hallway, are your personal quarters. They form the outside of the building and have windows. Each of you have been assigned your personal room ... or two rooms for a married couple ... and you slept in those rooms last night. The personal quarters are labeled with your first names and your work room in the same manner along with your work titles.

"The hallway comes into the dining room on both the west and east sides. The elevator on the west side adjacent to the kitchen can be used by our housekeeping and cooking staff only to access the storage room. The elevator on the east side can be accessed by anyone to the gym on the floor below us by way of fingerprint recognition. I assume you read the footnotes on the blueprints regarding access to the control room, the vehicles and weapons room, as well as access to the storage room. Those areas have limited access to those folks who need to be there.

"There is a fingerprint pad on the door to your quarters. Once that system is activated you will need to use it to gain access to your personal quarters, your work room, and the wall safe in your personal quarters. Should the need arise to occupy the compound, bring important documents with you to store in the safe ... or anything else that will fit. Do not bring any personal weapons ... rest assured there are more than enough weapons on the premises to go around ... just in case we might need to defend the house ... and enough ammunition to start a small war.

BLACK SNOW ... by Anne Rushton

"Any questions before we start our tour? If you have none now I am sure you will have some as we go along ... feel free to ask ... after all, this will likely be your home at some point for who knows how long."

CHAPTER 30

"We will start in here ... there aren't any false doors or walls ... no trap doors ... nothing gimmicky about the whole house really ... very straightforward. The only thing you might have missed are the four hidden security cameras ... one in each corner. Each of the work rooms have the same security cameras, along with the hallways, and the common areas. They aren't there to spy on you, but to protect you in the very unlikely event someone else would penetrate our substantial security. We do not have security cameras installed in your personal quarters for obvious reasons."

Moving to the dining room, they all took particular note of the convex south facing wall of LAMEX as well as the three feet of panels which were solar collectors. They made a brief stop in the kitchen which was equipped with some unusual appliances, but were assured everything to prepare and store food had been installed. Returning to the hallway, Ben pointed out the elevator and moved on. Just as Ben had said, the personal quarters were on the left and their work rooms were on the opposite wall.

Genevieve and Fawn's quarters were first in the hallway closest to the kitchen. "Their work rooms will be used for menu planning and keeping an inventory of their kitchen supplies and which ones must be brought from the supply room by elevator each day. Feeding a group this size three meals a day is no easy task. Each of them will serve as back up for the other in case of illness."

Elliott's work room on the right was the first door Ben opened and he went on to say "this will be the communications center manned by Elliott. He will be communicating with the outside world. The Federal Government has allowed all of the compounds to use one dedicated communications satellite. We will be able to communicate with the other compounds thru an encryption system which cannot be breached or detected. Elliott will give us a printed update of world events after dinner each night ... which will include information about not only the event which brings us here, but how this country and others are responding to it. Elliott's work room also houses the PA system. He will be able to communicate with any individual within the compound ... or make announcements throughout the entire house."

Ben closed the door and continued on with the tour. He pointed out each occupant's quarters and opened the door of their work room. "Polly's work room will be what I call a 'grooming' station, along with all her supplies and facilities for manicures and the weekly massages she has promised. I just had a thought ... who is going to do those things for you Polly? Sorry Polly and everyone ... just trying to interject a little humor and break the tension ... poor timing. In the unfortunate event Polly becomes ill, I suppose we will just fend for ourselves and have long hair until she recovers."

"My quarters and those of the security team are the last four rooms on the east before we enter the dining room.

BLACK SNOW ... by Anne Rushton

As you can see, each of our work rooms is stocked with a wall of security monitors, continually scanning inside the common areas of the house as well as the grounds outside. The four of us will take rotating six hour shifts. The three on the security team will also make a visual inspection of the vehicles and weapons areas on a daily basis. As a back up, an alarm will signal each of us four if anyone other than the authorized occupants are on the grounds or in the house. We four will meet in Drake's work room to review the situation and determine a proper course of action.

"My watch and stomach and smells from the kitchen tell me it is lunchtime. We have finished touring the top floor ... or living quarters and find ourselves once again back in the dining room just in time. Please form a casual line, serve yourselves from Genevieve's bounty."

CHAPTER 31

After lunch they moved to the floor below by a staircase built as a back up in case all the power was exhausted. The group moved first into the gym which contained everything imaginable for keeping fit or entertainment ... even a basketball court and billiards table.

They entered the storage area through a connecting door which opened and slid into the wall by way of a magnetic device Ben held. There was an audible gasp as the group surveyed the volume of supplies required to maintain a house of this size for two years. Each wall contained floor-to-ceiling shelving and the center had two additional rows of shelving back-to-back. All the racks of shelving were protected by wire cage doors to prevent the contents from spilling onto the floor. Three of the walls and the center aisles were given over to food storage, each shelf labeled as to contents and amounts. Several large upright freezers were located on the back wall between shelving. They could see that virtually all the food was either frozen, canned, powdered or dehydrated, to be reconstituted with water when needed. The fourth wall of shelves near the convex wall of LAMEX contained linens, towels, soap, detergent, hygiene products and cleaning products.

Ben elaborated on the food and linens section. "During the time we would live here, the connecting door between the gym and storage area would be locked and could only be opened by a magnetic device kept by our security people. Same thing applies to the west elevator from the first floor. It wouldn't recognize your fingerprint to bring you to the storage area; however, you are free to use the east elevator to come down to the gym any time you want. You wouldn't want to take any of those food products for your own use anyway. Only Genevieve and Fawn know how to turn these unappetizing cans and bags into something not only edible but tasty and nutritional.

"As for the linen supply, our housekeeping team of Claudia, Jo and Amber will distribute them according to your needs. They will launder bed linens and towels in their work rooms and restock your bathrooms. You will be responsible for your personal laundry ... you may not have noticed the washer and dryer combination located behind your bathroom door. You will also be responsible for keeping your work room and private quarters clean and orderly. The house has a built in whole house vacuum system with a connection located in each room on the wall. The hose and attachments are in one of your cabinets. Polly has a more than adequate supply of makeup and toiletries for the women in her work room. Of course you are free to bring your own if you wish, but be sure you bring enough to last up to two years.

"Now let's move down to the west side of the basement ... this will be the only time all of you will be able to visit that area ... except of course for myself, Ethan and Winston our hydrologist. This is the heart and soul of our compound and much of what you see will be a mystery as to how things work ... just trust that it does.

The elevator door opened to reveal what could only be described as an organized spider web of pipe, wire, gauges, telemetry devices, monitors and machinery. Ben pointed out the hanging signs designating the various areas ... one for Solar, one for Water, one for Fuel Cells, one for Water Conversion, one for Air Conditioning, one for Ventilation, one for Fuel Conversion. He was right ... most of the group had a blank stare on their face.

"I think it appropriate we all have a very simple, basic understanding of what and how this room works to assure you of your safety and comfort. I'll ask Ethan, the architect of all you see here, to discuss what I would call Basic HVAC 101."

"Well Ben, I think first we need to define HVAC which stands for heat, ventilation and air conditioning ... some of the basic needs we all have to live in comfort indoors. Consider this room one giant generator. We are totally off the electric grid ... which also helps to keep us invisible. Heat will come from fuel cells which store the sun's energy 24/7 regardless of the weather. Our system can even capture some of the sun's energy reflected from the moon at night. As long as the sun exists, we will have an unlimited amount of energy for our use. Moving on to air conditioning, it works the same way as heating, but in reverse. Ventilation is a simple exchange of fresh air for stale, oxygen depleted air. We can't depend on using outside air for this purpose in the event of a nuclear or biologic war, or volcanic eruption. What we can depend on is the oxygen contained in water ... the 'O' in H_2O. Our hydrologist can explain that. Winston, you are up next."

"Thank you Ethan for keeping it short. I know all our minds are boggled at this point, so I will try not to add to it anymore than necessary. What is our water source? It is a very deep well which brings water to the surface under this floor to prevent any contamination from the air. The motor for this is in that large container in the corner. Part of that water is shuttled off to holding tanks ... also underground ... for use in the house. Water quality in those tanks is maintained to perfect potability so you can drink from any faucet. Even your shower and laundry water is pure. The monitors for water purification are in my work room and are monitored 24/7. If I am sleeping and something needs my attention, a monitor on my night stand alerts me. What happens to the other part of the water? It passes through a complex process which splits each molecule of water into hydrogen and oxygen. The hydrogen is stored in fuel cells; the oxygen is either stored in a holding tank or introduced into the house as fresh air.

"Systems carefully monitor the level of carbon dioxide and when they indicate a replenishment of oxygen is needed, it is done automatically. Detectors are installed in each room of this house to monitor the air quality. Here again, if any of them alert, I receive a signal on a monitor I wear all the time. I can manually adjust these systems from my work room.

One subject we haven't covered is the one no one wants to bring up ... the disposal of sewage. As environmentally unsavory as it sounds, we have a sewage disposal system a significant distance south of the house, down the hill, which empties directly into the water we extract for drinking. Simple gravity keeps to two sites from ever mixing. Any questions? Ben, I guess it's back to you now."

"Our final stop will be the area for vehicle and weapons storage. This way please." Ben led them through the connecting door. The room seemed so much larger than Elliott remembered when he was here briefly upon his arrival. He didn't have a clue where he was then or what was about to unfold.

Drake stepped up and began to speak. "You will notice we have a number of vehicles here of various types. Nothing that looks like military, but we do have vehicles for rugged terrain travel, traditional armor plated limousine cars, a twenty passenger bus, even snowshoes. Notice a wall on the north side which separates the garage from the weapons room. We can take a look at that now.

Drake and Ben gained entry by fingerprint recognition ... any two of the four had to be present to gain entry to the weapons room.

"What you see before you are a variety of military weapons ...AK-47s, rifles, shotguns, pistols, laser and taser weapons, ammunition of all types and of sufficient quantity to defend our fortress adequately unless the entire Army comes on the property. Next week we will demonstrate the use of each weapon and train each of you in its use. All of you have had some experience with either a rifle or pistol, so we will focus most of our training on the ones you haven't used. We also have four suits of LAMEX, four suits of Kevlar, and twenty haz-mat suits in the unlikely event we needed to evacuate the house. You will be instructed in their use as well next weekend."

Ben held up his hand to quiet the murmuring among the group and asked them to return to the gathering room by way of the east elevator, with him leading the way.

CHAPTER 32

Elliott was the first to speak, directing his remarks to Ben. "Ben, I think I speak for the group when I say we are all more than impressed with what you have put together here ... all the amenities ... the defense mechanisms ... the actual structure. I for one feel very fortunate to perhaps benefit from all you have done. I hope I can measure up to your expectations should the need arise."

When Elliott finished speaking the entire group rose to applaud in agreement.

"Appreciate the sentiments Elliott ... and everyone else. While we might be very pleased with ourselves about what we have accomplished at this compound and the others, it is the means to an end. We might think about it like insurance ... it gives us a sense of comfort to have, but hope we never have to use it.

When you really think about the reasons the compounds were built, it becomes a very sad and sobering conversation we have with ourselves. For years America ... and the powers that be ... has wallowed in passive wanton destruction of our planet. The time to pay the bill is likely very near. There is always a price ... it just depends on when it has to be paid.

"I don't want to rush you off, but it is late afternoon and most of you have travel deadlines to meet. As I told you before, I live here now ... Ethan and Winston are staying this week. You will be expected to return next weekend, following the same schedule you had for this weekend. For those of you with flight tickets, be sure to do online check in and be prepared to meet your driver at the airport on either Friday night or Saturday morning early.

"Since Genevieve has made meal preparations for those of us who are staying, she has prepared enough for you to take a meal so you eat en route to your home destination.

"On Saturday each of you will spend the day in your work room familiarizing yourself with every button on every piece of equipment, testing it and testing yourself in its use. Each of you will be taken to the weapons room, one at a time, and given a short course on the use of all the firearms and clothing. The first half of Sunday, you will go to your work rooms and be prepared to operate in a simulated event in real time. During the afternoon, we will meet back here in the gathering room to discuss questions you have, report any problems or glitches, and dispense final instructions for occupation of the compound during an emergency. We will discuss what will constitute an emergency and who will issue the order to gather. I think that concludes the weekend and I wish you safe travel this evening and next weekend ... I will see you then.

"Remember to take nothing from the compound except your experience and memories of what you have learned this weekend ... and share them with no one. All of our lives depend on your silence."

CHAPTER 33

Elliott and Margaret suffered from sensory overload after they got home in Jacksonville and staggered through the following week barely able to function at work. What had started as a simple 'yes' to Joshua and Janice during one of their get togethers, was now life altering. Whether they ever gathered at the compound, they would all spend the rest of their lives on high alert.

In an imperceptible way, Elliott had begun moving into a very dark corner of his mind. He had slowly become aware that regardless of all the questions people were asking, the response he would have had to give was 'no'. It was so obvious, but so typical of the human population ... not a character flaw exactly ... but a desire and need to maintain the status quo. They didn't want to hear from researchers, scientists and the governments ... least of all committees of anything ... that the weather just might not get any better.

They both struggled through the days leading up to their second weekend at Jardin. Elliott and Margaret talked about it at night ... how they had already let go of their current lives and moved away from the 'if' into the 'when' stage. Each took turns reassuring the other they were doing the right thing. They had deep unanswered questions of the moral issues of saving only a few people from catastrophe ... and at times riddled with guilt that they were two of them. They had to keep reminding themselves and each other that it might not ever come to that ... but as a scientist, Elliott knew better. It was for Margaret's sake he played along with that little charade.

He had long since given up teaching directly ... deferring those duties to his assistants. They could always regenerate his teaching videos from earlier days at the University. His name and knowledge still endowed the University with respect so they pretty much let him chart his own course. He continued working with NOAA in an advisory capacity and that was claiming more and more of his time. The demand for his writing in academic publications had increased, but his contributions decreased. He simply couldn't bring himself to report on his real findings ... that Mother Nature seemed to have a self destruct button stuck in the 'on' position.

Elliott also knew what he wrote could cause mass panic and that was not an acceptable alternative either. He stopped accepting speaking engagements for the same reason. Word started to float around that he was ill which was a perfect cover for him. He looked gaunt and tense all the time and that fueled the fires of gossip even more. Good. He had no idea who at NOAA knew about what he came to think of as the 'fail safe' plan of the compounds. In the beginning Ben had said there were nine ... who knew how many there were now. He wasn't privy to that information and he really didn't want to know.

Finally, the weekend. Margaret and Elliott followed the same pattern as they had done before. Arriving in Atlanta, meeting their driver and arriving at the compound. Could it have been only a few days since they were there for the first time? This time there were no surprises about the 'cloak of secrecy' or anything else.

They were escorted to their room, asked to admit themselves by fingerprint identification and felt a strange familiarity in their surroundings. Drake had picked them up late Friday evening and asked them to help themselves to refreshments in the gathering room. Breakfast would be served at 7:00 A.M.

CHAPTER 34

Everyone served themselves from the buffet style they had become accustomed to as they entered the dining room. Some had finished eating, some just starting, and others such as Ben had yet to join them. The ones there didn't attempt polite social conversation ... the reason they were there was unmistakably grave. Elliott wondered if their week had been as tense as his and Margaret's.

Ben emerged with a hearty 'welcome back' to everyone as he proceeded to serve himself as well. After he sat down he took notice that all were back in their intended place. "Difficult week for everyone I would imagine" was his only comment except to direct them to the gathering room following the meal and added "bring your coffee if you want".

Once everyone was seated Ben stood and broke the silence. "Last week you all had a chance to meet, or hear from, or interact with, everyone on our team except for Samuel. As you should remember from the initial introductions Samuel is not only a Clinical Psychologist, but a retired military Chaplain. He is our spiritual advisor and will also help us walk through the mine field of psychological imprisonment once we are here for the duration. I want him to speak to you now."

Somewhat tall, he possessed a handsome physique and the ramrod straight stance of a military man. Grey hair appeared at his temples and he was a striking figure. Dressed casually now, Margaret thought he would make an imposing figure if he had come in his dress military uniform. She had to resist the urge to slap herself ... what a juvenile thought at such a serious occasion. Elliott had no doubt that Samuel could hold his own in any conversation or confrontation and it made Elliott like Samuel before he spoke his first word.

"This is not the customary group I am used to addressing, so I don't have any type of pre-planned speech. Truth be told, this is the most unique setting I have ever found myself in during my life. My hunch is that all of you feel the same way. I am a psychologist so I understand human nature. I am a Chaplain so I understand spiritual nature. At times these two things do battle with each other. At times the spiritual side of a person can help the human side ... to endure ... to make the right choice ... to accept an almost insurmountable challenge. That is what I think we all face here.

"I'm not asking for a show of hands, but during this past week did any of you experience a sense of withdrawing from your 'normal' world? Did you feel any sense of guilt about being singled out? Were you depressed at any time? Did you shed tears over what the human race is facing? Did you fear for your life and others in a deep gutteral way? I would bet all of you experienced all of those things during the past five days. Withdrawal is a defense mechanism; guilt comes from a sense of morality; depression is acknowledging reality in the face of adversity; crying is an outward sign of inner compassion or turmoil; fear is a natural experience to a sudden, unknown set of circumstances. Like coming across a bear in an otherwise bucolic forest ... that is stark white terror. Being a Chaplain I have seen all these emotions and more coming from the strongest men and women to wear a uniform. It isn't a sign of weakness; it is a sign of being human, and we can be no more than that. This time worn phrase is still true ...'it isn't how many times you get knocked down that counts, it is how many times you get up and go on'.

"The next thing I want to talk to you about comes from the Chaplain part of me ... religion and prayer. I am sure some of you are squirming in your seats about now. We have been so brainwashed that we fear hearing those words spoken aloud in a crowd. It is not 'politically correct' as they say. I don't let little people with small locked minds stop me from speaking about those things. God. See ... I said it and no one passed out. You have one ... a God ... whether you believe in Him or not; He still believes in you. He endowed you with life and the gifts you have been using in real life and the ones you will use here. No one is egotistical enough to think they have their gifts by their own doing. They have only acknowledged and taken advantage of the ones they were given to become a success in life.

"Prayer. See, I said another word you aren't used to hearing. Let me assure you of one thing ... when someone is in a foxhole with live ammunition flying overhead from the enemy, they learn how to pray real fast. One thing I have found myself telling people more than anything else is 'if there is no God and you pray, you've lost nothing; if there is a God and you don't pray, you've lost it all'.

"I want each of you to consider my work room a sanctuary. Come to me any time with any thought and with any feeling that is getting in the way of your day-to-day life here at Jardin. I think we have all come to accept the fact that it will not be a matter of 'if', but 'when'. The 'if' ship has already sailed."

Ben stood up to speak as most the others were seen dabbing at the corner of their eyes. "I can't say I know what each of you are feeling now ... Samuel said it for me. Thank you Samuel ... I will never be embarrassed to come knocking on your door. Incidently, did you all notice that Samuel had a small magnetic sign on his door during the tour last week? A green sign means he is available; a red sign signals he is in conference with someone ... don't knock ... just come back.

"I think we are ready to begin again. Please go to your work stations and begin your exploration. Genevieve will ask Elliott to announce lunch on the house intercom to give him practice with that part of his job. I will be by to see each one of you more than once today and get a report on your setup."

With that they each left the gathering room as they had entered ... stressed ... but perhaps a little less so thinking the whole group shared a lot of the same feelings.

CHAPTER 35

The remainder of the morning Ben made rounds as promised, answered questions, helped fix some glitches or overlooked procedures. After a successful whole house announcement of lunch by Elliott, everyone ate and returned to their work. The afternoon went more smoothly, especially for Elliott, Margaret, Winston, Drake, Leah and Jamison ... the ones who were most involved with technical operations. Ethan put his systems through the paces on the computer and checked that each back up or fail safe procedure worked as planned.

After Drake felt comfortable with all of his security checks and the automatic functions controlled by computers, he began taking each person to the weapons room for training.

Elliott was still setting up connections with the other compounds through their dedicated communications satellite when Genevieve asked him to announce that dinner would be served in thirty minutes. He was glad for the break, but knew he still had a lot to do the following day. After dinner Ben asked them to meet in the gathering room for an analysis of the day's events.

Each person gave the group a report of what they had done and the glitches they encountered which had all been resolved. Ben had been asked many questions during the day ... many of which were of a general nature and he said he wanted to answer them with the group together. He started down his list of notes.

"I realize we made an omission in our tour and that was the underground bunker where personal vehicles would be stored and I thank whoever brought it to my attention. Sometimes we get so wrapped up in the technical part of this project, we overlook something very simple. If you drive your car to Jardin we will be watching for you and open the gate from Drake's work station. Stop after you enter the gate and you will be able to see an open overhead door to the west of the house. That opening will lead you to the underground bunker. There are carts waiting for you to load your belongings on and a prominent overhead sign will direct you to the tunnel leading to the house. You will find an open elevator waiting to bring you into a small room adjacent to the kitchen and from there you can find the way to your quarters.

"What should I bring when I come to the compound? Enough casual comfortable clothing for two weeks. Although our plan now is that no one will have a need to ever go outside, bring a winter coat and other warm clothing that can sustain you during a time our heating system may be down for repairs. As I mentioned before, bring important documents for your safe. By that I mean a deed to your home, any insurance policies you have, birth certificates, marriage licenses, stocks and bonds, credit cards and checkbooks. Why credit cards and checkbooks? You certainly won't need them here, but why risk having someone steal them from your home?

"Money, yes. Some of you may feel more comfortable closing out bank accounts and converting money to travel checks. Bring pictures and any type of ornamentation you want to dress up your living quarters. I might suggest you pack suitcases as soon as you return home with the items I have mentioned. Make a list of the other things to grab when you need to come back here quickly. I might also suggest scaling down your lifestyle as much as you can now ... cancel unneeded credit cards, consolidate cash accounts, do whatever you can to burglar proof your home. If you have a second car, lock it in your garage before you come and bring the keys with you. Bring any regular medication you take and try to stockpile some of it in the meantime. There are ways of doing that ... this time you need to avail yourselves of those avenues.

"If you would be coming by car, make sure it stays fully charged at all times and be very diligent about regular maintenance ... one thing you don't want to have is a break down on the way here.

"What should you not bring? Weapons as we discussed before, any type of personal communications devices, alcoholic beverages, audio or video recording devices."

"One thing we didn't cover last week was garbage or trash. Whatever you call it, everything disposable you use here is biodegradable. Tissue, paper of any kind, paper napkins, so forth ... it all disintegrates when it comes in contact with water. Claudia will empty your trash cans into a collection bin, it will degrade the products with water and be flushed along with sewage from our bathrooms. As for food waste, there should be very little of that since Genevieve prepares meals very carefully. Whatever is left will go into an old fashioned garbage disposal machine and likewise be flushed."

The one question no doubt everyone had on their mind but didn't ask was about was the 'end game strategy'. Each person had been part of this group for a different reason, but one thing they all shared was intelligence that they used to succeed in life ... at least by now outdated definitions of 'success'.

Elliott felt compelled to ask the question.

"Ben, I think we all have one unasked and unanswered question ... what exactly do you have in mind as the 'end game strategy'?"

Ben looked around the room and could see that Elliott was right. He decided this was as good a time as any to open Pandora's box. After shuffling in his seat in contemplation, he said "I suppose that is up for grabs at this point. We don't know the event which will bring us together, so we can't make those plans ... and I haven't. If some isolated event occurs which turns Jardin into a haven for our group, then we have a good chance of re-emerging and re-assimilating into our current way of life with no one being the wiser.

BLACK SNOW ... by Anne Rushton

"My research associates have told me that the most likely event will be weather related ... or to be more precise, climate related. Now, everyone here knows what is going on with that ... global warming actually started being noticed by a small group of scientists during the 1950s. It didn't garner national and international attention until the early part of this century. Now it seems to take top billing in the news outlets at least once a week. Remember that when you are contacted and someone tells you it is the 'real deal', it is time to gather at Jardin for who knows how long.

"I have never wished for a crystal ball more than I do now."

CHAPTER 36 ... 2040

Once they returned home after their second weekend at the compound ... or Jardin as Ben preferred to call it ... both Elliott and Margaret were exhausted emotionally. At times they doubted their own sanity. Being able to distinguish reality from fiction, fact from theory, was becoming harder to do. Still, they shared none of their double life with anyone ... they were sworn to secrecy... and in addition they realized they would be looked upon as fools or part of a fringe group ... perhaps even suspected terrorists. They were in this club for the long haul and while in the beginning it had been flattering and somewhat comforting to become part of the Compound Project, now it began to consume much of their emotional energy. Elliott realized that Joshua and Janice had been wise to retire when they did ... should he and Margaret do the same? His work was consuming him emotionally and mentally ... he needed to leave it on someone else's shoulders but he knew he couldn't.

Elliott was perplexed that people just didn't 'get it'. Global warming which had first been noted nearly a century earlier ... with little notice paid to it ... had continued to worsen since that time until now, all the cards in the deck had been dealt and nobody had a winning hand. Not even he and Margaret ... nor Ben ... nor any of the others who would gather at compounds. Why were they gathering? The stock answer they all used was to 'wait it out'.

BLACK SNOW ... by Anne Rushton

In spite of all her accomplishments in the fields of education, health care, elected officials, environment, becoming a somewhat isolationist country, managing to balance the Federal Budget for the first time in many decades ... President Nelson couldn't control the one thing that could or would wipe out all her efforts .. the climate change. Oh yes, she had mandated strict emission policies and threw tons of money toward researching and implementing a very low national carbon footprint. Things had gotten done during her eight years in office simply because she had demanded it and cut off the source of a lot of what stood in the way of real progress by doing away with lobbyists and their self enrichment agenda.

All these progressive programs had enthralled the American population and polls continued showing an upswing in her approval rating. Finally the 98% had ... for the most part ... regained control of the country. The percentage of the middle class began to appear on reports in higher numbers each time. The locomotive was back on the right track and had started to chug faster and faster down the line to self sufficiency.

What could go wrong? Elliott did have an answer for that ... the climate change taking place before their eyes. All that had been done to make life better was basically too little, too late. He thought of it as an alcoholic, overweight smoker at age 60 who decides he is going to get rid of all the bad habits and replace them with good ones. The damage had been done and no one in the scientific community had a clue how to speed up the healing process ... if there indeed was one ... for either the man or human civilization.

Elliott knew in his heart that there was no end game. Once they went into the compound, it was likely they wouldn't come out. The climate could only worsen over time. Mother Nature didn't have a set of breaks that could stop this runaway train. Like it or not, Elliott knew that he and Margaret, and all the others, would likely spend the rest of their lives there. It was a chilling thought that he shared with no one but the demons in his mind.

Elliott went thru the motions of day-to-day life on autopilot from then on. He still held on to enough rational thinking to realize his life depended on that. In spite of what he knew, he couldn't tip his hand to anyone ... even Margaret. If he showed signs of even one of the demons in his mind, he knew that he and Margaret would be barred from the compound. That was their only chance of surviving what was to come.

CHAPTER 37

After the second group gathering at the compound for a 'dress rehearsal', Margaret herself had begun to move away from reality. One day she found herself lost in thought at the law firm. She made herself appear just busy enough to look engaged, but not so busy she couldn't think deeply about life and its true meaning. After all, that is why she and Elliott had joined the Compound Project ... for the safety of their own lives and an opportunity to help in some way salvage their knowledge to contribute to whatever life was left on the outside. She had always loved the concept of the legal system in this country. As flawed as it was, it was better than any other. It had been crafted bit by bit by men ... and eventually women ... who dared to take a stand in the face of opposition from the British Crown to segregate and liberate themselves from arbitrary foreign rule and form their own lifestyle ... every part of it.

The forefathers of this country, as they were commonly called, were flawed and fought among themselves ... but in the end they always united in the common good of mankind. That concept had drawn her into this profession ... those lofty ideals ... the pure motives. The early laws were put into place in the form of the Constitution, its Amendments and the Bill Of Rights. The country which for so long operated on those simple concepts had long since vanished. She had become disillusioned in recent years by the degradation of the brilliant thinking among early Colonists into

156

what had become little more than a free-for-all among the lawmakers and law enforcers. The lawyers were supposed to uphold their part of the equation ... simply to administer the laws and defend the rights of individuals. In many ways even that had been reduced to a beauty pageant or a spitting contest.

Margaret carried some Florida Statute books as props and walked to the back of the long hallway toward the Law Library. In a way that was a silly thing to do ... no one used those books anymore ... everything was searched electronically ... but the library did serve as window dressing to impress clients and a big conference table in the middle of the room was used to conduct negotiations and depositions ... even attend distant hearings by Skype. She walked slowly, passing each set of offices. Margaret looked at each person she saw ... really looked at them ... and wondered if they would ever convene in this configuration again.

She saw Senior standing in front of his tall windows, contemplating the light drizzle of gusty rain starting to fall. Junior's door was closed as usual ... but through his glass sidelight Margaret saw him diligently studying his computer screen and taking notes. She couldn't see what he was writing ... didn't matter; she knew what it was ... current stock prices. The Dow had lost half its value four years before in 2036. Rich folks with market investments lived or died by the market. Ending the day a few pennies up was cause for celebration ... which on a Friday after work meant drinks all around at the local watering hole. Margaret often thought if that place burned down on a Friday evening, it would take most of the lawyers and half the support staff in her firm with it.

William's office was next. The most arrogant of the arrogant. She had long since learned that arrogance was a necessary trait to becoming a successful attorney. They would say it was 'self esteem'. So far as it went with clients, that was true. The more self assured a lawyer was with a client, the more impressed the client was that they were in capable hands. But that layer of superiority should be left at the door at the end of a work day. William wore it like an entitlement all the time, regardless of whose presence he was in ... except when Senior came into his office and made a 'ahem' noise to announce his presence. William didn't look away from his computer as Margaret passed. He never considered anything important enough to take his time that he didn't personally allocate.

Maddox was the workhorse of the group. Truly dedicated to this clients and to making himself a partner before age thirty. He came to work early, often snacked thru lunch, almost always stayed late and never left the office without a stash of work in his bulging briefcase. As the keeper of such records, Margaret knew that Maddox always turned in the most billable hours each week. She thought it was good he had never made time in his life for finding a mate or having a family. He was married to the law and was a driven man.

Felicia seldom mixed or mingled among the other attorneys in or out of work. She was the firm's trial attorney and as such, was always elbow deep in researching precedent cases, current law, appellate decisions ... and putting the opposing counsel under a microscope. When she entered a court room, she was in top form and fully prepared. Most of the cases she took on ... and won ... were evidence based and not heavily dependent on witness testimony except by way of deposition or video interview. People couldn't always be trusted to tell the same story in Court as they once had, but documents didn't change. Just entering middle age, Felicia benefitted from all her years of practicing before the court, and projected an air of confidence and assertiveness seldom seen in a woman so beautiful, well groomed, dressed and coiffed by the finest in their fields. In fact that was often the very thin edge which won her cases. The opposition often viewed Felicia as a fashion statement, and by doing so, severely underestimated her abilities.

Chester, who did nothing but real estate and probate, was as dry and boring as his fields of practice. He punched in, did his work, and punched out. His billable hours stayed the same within an hour or two, week after week. Chester was the 'bread and butter' of the firm. The partners certainly didn't keep him on board because of his personality; it was always the bottom line they looked at. Margaret thought to herself that he could have slept thru the real estate closings and probate proceedings. An experienced legal assistant or paralegal did all the paperwork involved because it was so repetitious. All he had to do was meet with the clients, take a few notes and pass the notes along to one of the support staff to work on. He would review the files before the property closings to make sure everything was in order and then show up with papers to sign.

All the others were nameless faces or faceless names she worked with every day. They were on the second floor and except for their coming and going she never had reason to encounter them. In that sense it was a cold environment in which to work. That was fine with her ... getting chummy wasn't part of her job description or her style. The firm never engaged in anything as frivolous as a holiday party and if someone new came on board to replace someone who had left, they were introduced in the same informal way she had experienced ... a ten minute gathering in the conference room, a brief introduction, a group welcome, then everyone went back to work.

Margaret felt sure that Jessica, the bookkeeper, was cooking the books in some way. She just didn't have any proof of it but more and more the figures were not adding up the way they should.

CHAPTER 38

In the days and weeks that followed, all four now in the 'club' ... the Stewarts and the Adams, made every effort to return to their schedule and normal routine. They continued their weekly dinner meetings and the conversation was always about the project or the compound. It had become larger than life in their minds ... and closer than they wanted it to be. It was little more than a frail safety net woven from holes big enough for a cat to fall thru. Especially so since the remainder of that winter season in Jacksonville had become brutally cold with high winds and blowing snow ... something the four of them were seeing for the first time as Floridians.

According to Elliott the weather was, as he put it, 'off the charts' all over the country. Computers could still predict with accuracy what would happen where and when, but it was the upside down change that was really making people afraid. As the weeks and months wore on, more and more folks were looking up from their daily grind into the sky and wondering what was really going on. Was this just a freak of nature or was there more to it than that?

Because the jet stream was so far south, the western side of its bell curve lay across the northern mid west. The Dakotas, Nebraska, Kansas and states to the east of them had unusually warm temperatures and dry weather. It rained a lot, but the area on the high end of the bell curve received only trace amounts of snow. Snow was really the lifeblood of the 'market basket' as this area had been called for decades.

BLACK SNOW ... by Anne Rushton

The slow thaw of spring and snow melt into the soil provided groundwater for the crops of the coming season. Agribusinesses began to really wonder what kind of harvest they would have that summer, although in some ways they felt they already had summer during the winter months.

In March the jet stream which seemed to have been stuck in northern Florida slowly receded to the north, reversing the bell curve and returning about half the country to what was considered a 'normal' weather pattern. Cold and rainy or snowy 'up north' and hot and humid 'down south'. Elliott, the other three in the club ... and actually the whole of America breathed a collective sigh of relief. The relief was short lived.

The downside of the return to a more normal weather pattern was a tremendous outbreak of massive, dangerous and deadly tornadoes which lasted several weeks. The strength of the storms were, here again, 'off the charts' of measurement. Even the wind measuring instruments were destroyed or so severely damaged, meteorologists had to estimate the wind speed in some events. FEMA quickly deployed workers to those areas and the National Guard was called up to enforce civil obedience and an equitable distribution of the necessities of life. Over the past decade the decision had been made to decommission all designated above ground shelters and start building ones underground. Fortunately, about half the planned shelters were in place during that spring and people had no hesitation to use them when given instructions to evacuate. Many folks who could afford it and who lived on rural land returned to the 'bomb shelter' mentality of the 1950s and 1960s and built their own.

Elliott dreaded that summer in Florida for one reason ... hurricane season. As bad as the winter and spring months had been, it could only mean one of two things. Either the violent vortex of weather had spent itself with blizzards and tornadoes, or it was just a preview of things to come. May, June, July and August came and went with barely a whimper out of the Gulf Of Mexico or off the coast of Africa where hurricanes are born. He was hoping for the best for the rest of the 'season', but feared the worst.

His worst fears were confirmed when all of a sudden in the third week of October, it seemed out of nowhere a tropical depression formed in the Gulf Of Mexico and another was born in the Atlantic Ocean about halfway between Africa and Florida. They were both headed for the U.S. mainland. Forecasters put their computers into overdrive producing model after model of predicted landfall. Often times the European models differed, but this time an overlay of both models were almost exact copies. All the models had the Atlantic storm building to a Category 5 storm named Alicia and the Gulf storm doing the same thing ... becoming Hurricane Boris, gaining strength to produce Category 5 conditions. Alicia was headed straight for southern Florida, exiting into the eastern Gulf Of Mexico and actually combining with Boris to head due north in what could only be described as the 'storm of the ages'. Never in the history of storm tracking had two Cat 5 hurricanes collided and merged and not only maintained their individual integrity, but were locked together as one storm to continue tracking in the same northern direction. Elliott thought of the predicted outcome as a maniacal twisted dance of death the lovers Alicia and Boris were about to engage in.

The only blessing in the whole contorted mess was that the storms were almost 72 hours away from their collision. Alicia still had to cut a swath through Florida and that would be no small event in and of itself. She was going to be a Cat 5 when she made landfall over a huge land mass between Cocoa Beach and Miami. She might still be a Cat 4 when she exited the western edge of Florida. On the other hand, the models were showing her maintaining her wind speed as she cut a swath across the state. Alicia was enormous ... 150 miles in diameter ... and both sides of this whirling dervish would still be over water for a long time ... warm water which fed a hurricane's strength.

All eyes fell on Hurricane Boris ... if he made a northern turn fast enough and the air currents pushed him along fast enough, he would make landfall ahead of Alicia and avoid the collision. It would be devastating even under this 'best case scenario'.

The National Weather Service took over all broadcasting networks within the storms pathways and all local broadcasting was likewise replaced by weather announcements. Florida didn't have the luxury of building underground shelters as they had in the mid west because of the river of water which ran under the state called the 'Aquifer'. The only real survival strategy that could be implemented was evacuation ... but how to send over a million people out of harm's way at the same time was a logistics impossibility. Still they had to try. The order was given ... evacuate if you didn't have underground shelter.

Governors from all southern coastal states requested ... and received ... immediate deployment of National Guard Troops to implement an orderly evacuation. The 'safest' route and destination would be to the eastern seaboard ... coastal Georgia, South and North Carolina and the farther north the better. All models indicated this area would escape a direct hit or even a glancing blow of Alicia-Boris.

There had always been a running commentary by the Florida Visitor's Bureau that 'all roads lead to Florida'. This time all roads were leading out of Florida. All lanes of all interstate highways were ordered to become one way only ... effective within one hour. Everyone driving south of Atlanta and Savannah would be forced to exit and re-enter the interstate and drive north or use secondary highways to go south.

Elevated monorails running in the interstate median would continue running in both directions ... taking people north and returning to take more at over a hundred fifty miles an hour ... thus giving it the moniker of 'bullet train'. Same with the rail system ... all passenger trains in the south were regrouped to make similar runs. That left the airports to deal with and restructure flights. All aircraft located in Florida were grounded from continuing their normal schedules. The planes were ordered to transport people ... at the most 300 at a time ... to the shelter areas along the eastern seaboard.

In spite of early warnings and good implementation of FEMA's disaster plans put into motion, it still seemed impossible to get everyone to safe haven in time. Shelters and the necessities of life were ready and waiting to take in the evacuees. Some folks couldn't leave ... inmates in prisons and critical hospital patients ... they had to 'shelter in place' as best they could. There were always people who refused to leave, in spite of law enforcement orders ... so the police took their names, addresses and next of kin information.

The next set of hourly models Elliott and the team at NOAA ran showed a terrifying development. The bell curve of the jet stream was changing to resemble an undulating snake. Each hour sent the top of the bell curve higher and higher. To the west of the bell the curve had dipped so far down so as to nearly reach the Texas seacoast on the Gulf Of Mexico. This could only mean one thing ... the 'Siberian Express' was galloping south from Canada. The NOAA team watched in disbelief as the bell became tighter and more extreme. The atmospheric pressure indicated a strong warm and wet pattern was beginning to form in the mid west ...

tornadoes. Oftentimes hurricanes spun off tornadoes, but the conditions setting up for these tornadoes were not even related to the anticipated Mega Hurricane as they began to call the Alicia - Boris marriage.

The icing on the cake was spotted by NOAA later that same day ... to the west of the tornado alley scenario, an enormous western cold front was beginning to descend and the models predicted it would clash with the anticipated tornadoes. Alicia - Boris, tornadoes, torrential rains from all ... and now an ice or snow storm. Every weather pattern was continuing to undulate and there was absolutely no way of forecasting or making any kind of prediction ... except that all the factors were starting to come into place for an apocalyptic weather event the likes of which would affect two-thirds of the population and had never been observed or recorded in the history of modern man.

CHAPTER 39

Elliott called Margaret at work, which was odd. They had a long standing pact that neither of them would call the other on their private earbud unless it was really something that couldn't wait. This couldn't.

"Margaret, listen carefully, this is it. You know I wouldn't give you this signal unless it was the 'real deal'. You need to leave for home now ... say you won't be back this afternoon because of a blinding headache. This will give us a short head start on the others. With the weekend starting tomorrow, they won't know you are gone until Monday ... that is, the ones who show up for work Monday like the robots they are. Get your personal kit together ... our package of important documents ... you have the list we made of other things a couple of months ago ... and meet me at home. I will get the car fully charged and with any luck we can make the 350 mile trip by nightfall."

So this was it. Elliott and Margaret had made detailed plans for this day ... both hoping it would never come. They were better prepared than most folks as far as living necessities. The real test would be the emotional survival. Margaret realized with a start that sent cold shivers down her spine that she was totally unprepared mentally, but had no choice but to follow through. In all likelihood her own survival hung in the balance.

During the short time before she left the office, she stupidly but briefly entertained the thought of cleaning out her desk. She had to stop living in the 'normal' mode and switch on her 'new normal'. She went through her desk drawers one by one just looking at what she was leaving behind. She checked her filing cabinet drawers even knowing she had for a long time kept herself braced for this and kept detailed notes inside each case file annotating 'work done' and 'work to be done'. Not that it would matter. If Elliott was right, after today ... and the next day ... and the next week nothing would matter except just living. She imagined what life would be like then ... some of the 'suits' (as Elliott had jokingly called the lawyers) would still try to continue with business as usual. Honorable or stupid? Maybe both. Who knows how one would respond to the unexpected events totally out of our control and totally out of control until they happen.

Margaret quietly put Brenda's picture in her purse, put her suit coat on and left. As she closed the door and started for her car she knew everyone's life was about to change ... none more than hers. At least, she thought, I have a chance of making it out the other side of what was to come. Sadly, all the money the lawyers made together wouldn't be enough to buy them a warm blanket at the Mall.

CHAPTER 40

Margaret pulled her 'Brenda-blue' car into their garage, looked at the key as she put it in her purse and wondered how long it would be before she used it again. The image made her go numb. Better that than panic, she thought to herself. Inside she gathered the things on the list to take and left them near the door to the garage so Elliott could load them quickly.

Elliott arrived and began loading their cargo while Margaret took a last look at each room in their beautiful home. It had been her haven ... their haven ... and she wondered if they would ever see it or any part of it again. She couldn't help herself ... she broke down in sobs at the prospect of having yet another dream die a sudden death. Elliott found Margaret and helped her to the waiting car. They drove away and Margaret watched the house as long as it was in view.

Quickly Elliott accelerated the car once they were on the interstate heading north out of Jacksonville toward the compound northwest of Atlanta. For a long time neither of them spoke a word. They had been trained to live at Jardin, but no amount of training or preparation could help them deal with their emotions now. Best they not talk about what they had just left or their destination, or the purpose of their destination.

After driving about an hour, Margaret broke the silence between them. "Elliott, I love you."

BLACK SNOW ... by Anne Rushton

"I love you too Margaret. Somehow we will get through this and we WILL come out the other end."

"What was it Elliott ... what did you see that made you call the 'real deal' alert?"

"Actually Ben called me and said it was all over the news about two hurricanes converging and steam rolling into Florida's big bend and heading north. Don't worry, that won't actually happen for another 36 hours or so ... we have plenty of time to make it. Before Ben called me I was going to call him because we saw the early stage of a tremendous blizzard come out of Canada and all the models showed that it would collide with the mega hurricane somewhere in northern Alabama and the whole hellacious mess will supposedly drag east pushed by the jet stream. I don't even have a word in my weatherman's vocabulary of what to call something like that ... and neither does anyone at NOAA. This is a first for all of us. All we know is that it will be big, bad and devastating to the entire eastern third of the nation for who knows how long."

Elliott continued "if that wasn't bad enough, we started receiving reports today that the volcano under Yellowstone was showing significant seismic activity. If that thing blows, I can't even imagine what the landscape will look like in the western part of the country".

"So Ben doesn't even know about the Yellowstone thing yet?"

"No and when he learns about it, he will be reassured

that he made the right call to gather at the compound."

"Elliott, I wish I had given more thought and preparation for the emotional experience I am having right now. To tell you the truth, I am scared to death and I don't know if I can pull it together enough to do my work at the compound. I also wish I had taken the time to go to church and find strength in a greater power than myself ... I feel so helpless."

"Margaret, I think what you are going through right now is the same thing all the others are dealing with ... me included. What we need to do is pull together all the inner strength we have because other people are depending on us. We can make a difference for them as well as ourselves. I am going to get off at the next exit and get us something at a drive thru ... we need the energy and comfort of some warm food right now. Now that I think of it, cancel the drive thru ... we need to go in, go to the bathroom and rejoin civilization for a few minutes. A half hour won't make that much difference in our arrival."

A light rain was falling when they resumed their drive. "Elliott, do you want me to drive awhile?"

"I am fine ... lay the seat back and try to get a nap or just rest. There is no sense in us trying to pretend this trip is anything other than what it is ... but maybe somewhere deep down we can find a sense of gratitude for being part of the group. It won't guarantee our survival, but we have a heck of a lot better shot at it than ... well, others."

BLACK SNOW ... by Anne Rushton

Elliott channeled the radio to one of his ear buds hoping to listen to some calming music. All he could find were weather reports by excited drama queens ... or kings. He thought to himself what jerks some of these people are ... they are still trying to be the star of the show and get the ratings. Then he felt sorry for them. He turned the radio off. Obviously the big weather story had been leaked to the press by some headline seeker which was going to require FEMA, the Federal government, NOAA, Homeland Security and all the other agencies involved to leap frog ahead of the panic.

Traffic had been heavy south of Atlanta, but it always was ... and he noticed planes were still landing and taking off as he passed under the flight path of Hartsfield Airport. Elliott decided to take the more direct route thru the city ... it was past rush hour and he thought he could make better time that way.

Once they were north of Atlanta, he felt a sense of relief and dread at the same time. Relief they had navigated Atlanta without incident and dread that he was nearing the compound and would have to wake Margaret. She seemed to be in a deep sleep and he was sorry that when she woke, reality would set in again.

"Elliott ... where are we now?"

"Just about fifteen minutes south of the exit to the compound. I had hoped you could sleep until we got there ... how do you feel ... any better with some rest?"

BLACK SNOW ... by Anne Rushton

"Some. I think I had a panic attack Elliott ... I haven't experienced anything like that since Brenda died. The enormity of not only what we are facing, but more so for what tens of millions of unprepared people are facing. The death toll will be substantial, don't you think?"

"I'm sure that's something I'll be notified of in due time but I don't want to think ahead to that. For now we have to just get to the compound, get all our stuff to our quarters and take our cue from Ben. I think once we're safely inside the house and have our things around us, that should give us a small sense of relief we have made it this far ... away from the storm to come ... and it will give us a few days ... two at the most ... to really get a routine going."

Elliott nearly passed by the entrance to the compound ... stopped and backed up a little, and could see an invisible gate open. Following instructions, he drove to the dimly lit bunker and pulled in next to Joshua and Janice's car.

Once unloaded they made their way thru the tunnel, up the elevator and found their way into the house. Margaret and Elliott both commented they felt a sense of relief getting that horrible trip behind them. In a wistful way, he wondered when ... or if ... he would ever drive away from this place. No time for that nonsense ... they had to get settled in. They hadn't completely arrived yet and already he was starting to think of when they would leave.

Walking down the corridor, they passed Joshua and Janice's open door. Catching a glimpse of the Stewarts, they both came out and all had a group hug like long lost relatives at a family reunion. Elliott knew then the camaraderie among the people there would be just like that from then on ... like a family united in a common cause. Ben was right when he said early on there would be no titles or room for egos ... it would be one for all and all for one.

CHAPTER 41

"Janice and I got here about an hour ago ... how was the traffic ... did you listen to the radio ... some idiot reporter somehow got the scoop on what was going on with the storms and spilled it all over the networks. Now he is acting like a hero for telling the 'American people what they should know'. Bullshit ... all he did was start a panic. The Feds had already put the National Guard in place and they are directing evacuations now ... I wondered if you got tangled up in any of that traffic. I don't mind telling you that both Janice and I got a real case of nerves on the way here. We were both blind sided ... we thought we were ready for this ... and we were mechanically ... you know ... but we both had a hard time just making it up here. So good to see you ... meet us in the gathering room as soon as you dump your stuff in your rooms."

Elliott and Margaret looked at each other with a sense of sadness. They weren't happy that Joshua and Janice were about to come unglued, but it did give them some assurance that they weren't the only ones. When they got to their quarters, a strange sense of calm came over both of them. They had been there before ... twice ... and while it wasn't home, it wasn't a strange place to be either.

After everyone had arrived and had been directed to the gathering room, Ben came in. He went to everyone individually, hugged everyone and said "thank you". It wasn't a time to 'welcome' them ... it wasn't a festive atmosphere for that.   They all knew what he meant by his greeting. Genevieve and Fawn had the table filled with late night snacks. They had stocked the freezers with delicate pastries and fruits of all kinds for special occasions, and brought some of them out ... along with small sandwiches ... for the arrival.

"We all know why we are here so I won't belabor that point. I have been in constant communications with leaders of the other compounds for several days, debating the necessity of issuing the 'real deal' call and late yesterday morning we decided to put it in place. When we were all gathered here a few months ago, I pretty much knew we would meet again ... I just didn't think it would be this soon.

"When Elliott arrived he told me that after my call to him, he and NOAA were notified that the Yellowstone underground volcano was starting to alert increasing and significant seismic activity. Now, I and the other leaders are so glad we hit the call button. We should be prepared for just about every weather related event you could imagine ... except a clear sunny day. We are expected to be in the path of the mega hurricanes from the south, tornadoes that might spawn from them and go who knows where, a winter blizzard barreling across the mid west predicted to intersect the hurricanes in northern Alabama, and now the possibility of a volcanic eruption.

"Our compound and two others are in the cross-hair of the storms, and if Yellowstone does erupt there won't be a person in this country unaffected. We expect to have deteriorating conditions begin sometime on Sunday ... after that is open to debate. Rest assured Elliott will keep us posted. The only plan we have is to take care of ourselves and each other as best we can. No doubt we could suffer some calamity here at Jardin ... we'll deal with that if and when it happens. From now on we are in uncharted waters. There is no way anyone can plan for every contingency ... but I think we are pretty well covered here.

"Tonight we will all rest as best we can and go to our work rooms after breakfast at 7 A.M. Drake, Leah and Jamison already have the security system on automatic monitoring tonight, although I doubt seriously we will have any intrusion. Elliott, please check with the other compounds tomorrow to make sure everyone arrived and they are up and running according to plan. Let me know what you find out.

"We will be known as 'Compound 1' to the others, and they will be numbered in the order they came into our system. Incidently this entire project has been given the code name 'Operation Cornerstone' by the Feds and we may receive communications in that name from FEMA or other supporting agencies.

"Samuel, I imagine your services, in the way of support and encouragement, will be invaluable to us. Please dismiss us with a few words of comfort or prayer directed to whatever higher power each of you look to for guidance."

Margaret and Elliott left unpacking chores until the next morning and fell into bed exhausted. What had started out

BLACK SNOW ... by Anne Rushton

a normal day at work for Margaret had ended in a scene and at a place she hoped she would never be in. She realized Elliott must have had some suspicion of this day coming sooner rather than later since it was his information that confirmed the call to gather.

An eerie quiet fell over the house as everyone tried to come to terms with the uncertainty of what was to follow and find some inner strength to draw on.

CHAPTER 42

Ben stood up at the dining table after everyone had finished breakfast and asked Samuel to offer some words of thanksgiving and comfort. "I am going to be very politically incorrect and ask Samuel to say a prayer each morning before our work day begins asking for our safety and well being as we carry out our mission here. Any objections?" Everyone remained silent and bowed their heads. They needed all the help they could get ... remembering Samuel's earlier admonition that 'if there is no God and we pray, then nothing is lost; if there is a God and we don't pray, we've lost everything'.

Everyone thanked Samuel for his words ... either with a nod, smile or handshake. Elliott immediately got to work by bringing his computers and communications systems online. He was able to connect with the five compounds which were already activated and the remaining as they each came online. They all had made the 'real deal' call to gather. All the compound leaders had conferred Friday morning and it was a unanimous decision to make the call.

Margaret finished their unpacking and did her best to soften the barren look of their quarters with mementoes from home. She put Brenda's urn in the safe along with their vital records and a sizeable amount of money. She could delay no longer ... she had to cross the hall and begin the business of what she was brought there to do. It was like having 'new job jitters' she thought to herself. She first pulled out the book of instructions as to what records should be kept and how. She had already set up folders on her computer for that purpose and began making the daily entries. Because part of the compound project had been backed with government funds from the Black Budget, she had to keep abreast of all the activities at Jardin, and send daily reports to all the agencies involved.

One of her duties was to monitor and record each individual's daily participation. A copy of that report would be sent to FEMA, the controlling agency during an emergency, early the following day. During the day she was to journal all the events including any problems encountered and how they were dealt with and the people involved. She also maintained expenditure reports ... not in monetary terms, but of supplies. Genevieve or Fawn and Claudia gave her a list of items taken from the supply room downstairs at the end of each day and she would also send that report to FEMA. Most of her work would begin the following morning ... Sunday ... when she would compile and send reports from their first full day at the compound. In that sense, she was always working a day behind.

Elliott's work was similar as to reporting requirements, but his were limited to weather monitoring and reporting conditions at the compound. His work was more monitoring and maintaining contact with the other compounds than anything else. He was in charge of all the communications sent or received.

BLACK SNOW ... by Anne Rushton

Everyone was present and accounted for at all the compounds and were busy setting up routines ... except for one. During his connection with Compound 4 in Iowa, he learned that one of its members was a 'no show'. He immediately paged Ben. As Elliott was learning the details, Ben came into his room and closed the door. Elliott said "one no-show at 4 ... details are just coming in ... sit down and we can read it together":

" ... after the second weekend of training I was suspicious ..."

"Elliott, who are you talking to?"

"My counterpart in communications there."

" ... something just wasn't right ... not a good fit ... reported it to our leader after the second weekend of training who contacted DHS. Before they could put a sting operation in place, all of a sudden news reports began to come out concerning the impending weather catastrophe. He sat on the story until all Hell started breaking lose with the double hurricanes converging and decided to defect. They found out he had leaked the story ... for money ... to a media outlet. Was one of our security personnel ... DHS had him picked up last night and held in protective custody for reasons of national security, so he doesn't get a lawyer or a hearing until this event is over. They tried to bury the leak fast and instead they have focused on evacuation procedures and other emergency matters. They also picked up the reporter who bribed him and will hold him in a likewise manner."

"Elliott, ask him if the guy told the reporter anything about the compound project."

" ... don't really know at this point ... DHS is treating him like a terrorist ... interrogating him ... will let you know what we find out."

"Elliott, ask him how they are handling the situation as far as being short one member and how they will fill his job."

" ... our leader will step into an active security role as well ... the three will now work eight hour shifts monitoring security for the time being. DHS is going to send a member of the National Guard to fill in for the leaker."

Elliott sent a response asking to maintain contact throughout and keep their channel open so he could monitor their communications.

"Son-of-a-bitch ... sold us all down the river for a few bucks. What in Hell did he think he was going to do with it ... buy a sled?"

"Now Ben, we don't know that yet ... have to wait and see what DHS gets out of him. He may not have even mentioned the compound project. My guess is he didn't ... he just wanted to sell the storm story to the highest bidder ... he had nothing to gain and everything to lose by revealing the compound project ... he just thought he would sell the storm story and go on to the compound as planned. At least those are my thoughts."

"Makes sense Elliott, but they better run at high alert at '4' until they know for sure."

BLACK SNOW ... by Anne Rushton

Elliott tried to inject a little comic relief which Ben bought ... "at least it wasn't the cook" after he saw Genevieve slip a note under the door asking Elliott to call everyone to lunch.

CHAPTER 43

After returning to work ... without Ben at his side ... Elliott first checked the dedicated seismic monitor for activity in Yellowstone. His stress level jumped into a higher gear when he saw that it had increased from early morning. The White House had ordered a mandatory evacuation within a fifty mile radius of the Park the day before because of the oncoming blizzard ... now it included possible volcanic activity and they extended the evacuation to a hundred mile radius of the center of the Park. This was a formidable task since the Arctic blizzard had left snow ... knee deep in some places; waist deep in drifts.

The Park had been closed to visitors for over ten years, but a few Rangers were still there to monitor and maintain ... mostly keeping roads cleared of branches and fallen trees. They also issued periodic reports to the EPA on animal welfare. Today one the Rangers reported that wildlife had all but vanished. They said animals had a better sense of nature than man and no doubt their instincts told them to shelter in caves, under heavy brush or wherever else they could. The blizzard was starting to pass thru the Wyoming side of the Park, headed east.

Margaret stepped around the corner from her work room to Elliott's to get an update on the weather. "We should be seeing some early rain bands tomorrow morning, although the bad news is that the mega-storm has slowed on its march north. It had combined before making landfall in Florida's big bend and reports from that area are not good. Slowing down is giving the blizzard time to catch up. The entire state of Florida, including the Keys, has been declared in a state of emergency. Martial law has been imposed and curfews strictly enforced."

The President had just ordered broadcast television to be suspended with the Emergency Alert System taking its place in the entire eastern third of the country. Evacuation from Florida and Georgia to coastal areas was proceeding, although not without huge gridlock in places. The Guard was keeping the traffic moving, forcing breakdowns to the shoulder or grassy areas. The Highway Patrol was not issuing citations for wrecks or fender benders ... only taking down information of vehicles and passengers to be dealt with later. If vehicles were still able to travel, they were told to move on unless there was serious injury involved. The injured and their families were being airlifted by the Guard to the nearest hospital and their disabled vehicles just pulled off the road.

Drake was pulling his shift in security monitoring during mid afternoon when he noticed a car drive very slowly on the road down the hill in front of the compound. Since a 'DEAD END STREET' sign had been placed at the entrance to that road, Drake was in alert mode. Just to be on the safe side, he notified Elliott and they made a decision to call for back up. Drake called DHS to ask the National Guard to check it out. Some of the Guard had been stationed in cities or towns within ten miles of each compound, although they could be activated only by the DHS, FEMA or the White House. Drake felt some of the tension melt away when, ten minutes later, they saw a Guard vehicle pass the compound on the road. Except in crisis situations, the compounds were not notified of results of such a call. There simply wasn't enough manpower or time.

Things ran smoothly the rest of the afternoon, and Elliott felt like they were lucky not to have more events to deal with than they had. He called everyone to dinner at 7 P.M. with a message to go to the gathering room following the meal.

He put all his systems on auto-notify. As he stood and stretched, he realized the stress and adrenaline from the day had made him very tired.

CHAPTER 44

Leah was now working the security room so she was the only one missing from dinner. Ben asked Fawn to take her a meal while the rest of them served themselves and ate.

In the gathering room Ben asked each one to report on their day ... not only to keep everyone in the loop, but for Margaret's report she had to send the next day. "If you have nothing out of the ordinary to report, just say 'according to plan'. Elliott since you are in the first chair, we will start with you and go around the room."

Elliott first reported that he had linked to all the other compounds and their status. He outlined the events of Compound 4 being short one member and why. "I think you need to be aware of everything going on here and all the other houses. I guess on balance, only one defector from all the people involved is not a bad average ... but I remind you that we don't have any room for error in this project ... especially as the days pass and the weather starts to pummel all the compounds.

"Speaking of which I know you are anxious to get an update. The two hurricanes did merge before making landfall in Florida's big bend. That collision slowed their forward speed somewhat, but it also gave the storm time to intensify since most of it was still over water in the Gulf. The other bad factor about its slowed forward speed is that the western blizzard would have more time to catch up to it, so to speak. The mega hurricane now has sustained winds of 150 MPH and I don't need to tell anyone in this room what that means. At that strength it will destroy everything in its path. Tallahassee, Florida's capital, lies northwest of the big bend and has sustained substantial damage. Jacksonville, to the east, has sustained damage, but not to the extent of the capital. There aren't now, nor will there be, any immediate reports of casualties. The emergency response teams in place have a priority of assisting survivors once the storm passes far enough north to be safe to operate in. The peninsula of Florida sustained some damage from Hurricane Alicia as it passed over as a Category 3 hurricane on her way to meet up with Hurricane Boris in the Gulf of Mexico. No casualty reports yet or damage estimates from that.

"NOAA's best guess is that because the combined hurricanes are so enormous ... 300 miles in diameter and now maintaining one central eye wall instead of two ... we will begin to see light rain tomorrow from the outer bands. Once the rain begins, we can expect it to intensify, along with wind velocity. In the worst case scenario, the blizzard barreling across the mid section of the country will collide with the hurricanes and we will then enter uncharted territory."

Samuel asked "meaning what"?

"Meaning this event has never occurred in written history, so we don't know what to expect. The computers are so confused and confounded by this possibility they are continually crashing when NOAA feeds all this new data in. My best scientific prediction is that 'all Hell will break lose' ...

sorry Samuel." Samuel nodded.

"Not to add insult to injury, but the seismologists report that Yellowstone's volcano activity is increasing. FEMA issued an evacuation order for residents within a hundred mile radius of the Park which is no small feat in a blizzard and its aftermath."

Margaret, Joshua, Janice, Samuel, Jamison, Winston, Ethan, Polly, Genevieve, Fawn, Claudia and her team of Jo and Amber, and Leah by intercom all reported 'according to plan'. With the passage of a few hours, Drake felt the car driving by event was likely insignificant, but he still reported it to the group. "Did you record the vehicle make and model and license plate?" Jamison asked. "Yes, and we passed that data on to the DHS. That vehicle will be on their 'watch list' as well as ours. Elliott and I asked them for some back up, so ten minutes later I saw a National Guard vehicle go down the road in the same direction as the car. The road in front actually does dead end and no one occupies any property on either side. There was a reason the person driving the car came down this way ... we just don't know what it was. The DHS has a policy during a state of emergency of not revealing the results of a call, so we don't know what they found ... if anything."

"Hmm" Ben said ... "car goes down the road and doesn't come back ... Guard vehicle goes down the road and doesn't come back ... what could that mean?"

Absent any response Ben said "guess we just watch

and wait".

They didn't have to wait long. Leah reported by intercom that the vehicle they had reported just passed in front of the compound followed by the Guard vehicle.

"I want an answer Drake" Ben said ... "I think we have a right to know what happened during this interval."

"I'll contact them tomorrow morning early".

"No, now ... go contact them and we will wait for you" Ben insisted.

The group chatted among themselves while waiting for Drake to return, mostly about the adjustments they were making. Some seemed better able to make the transition ... mostly the ones whose profession required travel and adjustments to different environments such as Leah and Jamison.

Drake re-entered the room hoping Ben would accept what he had been told. "Obviously in this setting I can't offer any proof or guarantee what I have been told, but the DHS said the driver in the car was a realtor looking for acreage for a client and had made a wrong turn into our road. Evidently the Guard questioned her a long time which must have raised some suspicion in her mind. They checked her credentials and her story panned out, so they released her."

"Better safe than sorry" Ben muttered then redirected the conversation back to events of their first full day at the compound.

CHAPTER 45

The next morning after breakfast at Samuel's request they met in the gathering room for what some might consider a Sunday morning church service, although the protocol suggested nothing like that. Mostly, he wanted to offer a word of thanksgiving for their safe arrival and asked for courage from their 'higher power' to help each of them endure what was to come. He reissued his invitation to come to his work room any time they needed some help with their emotions. "This event is unprecedented in history ... and I want you to remember that I was a practicing psychologist for a very long time before I started my work as a Chaplain. We are all facing the unknown and we need to be in top form to work not only as individuals carrying out our responsibilities, but to work as a team if called upon." With that he thanked the group for their attention and said he would like to have a similar gathering each Sunday. He told them to feel free to suggest other things they would like to have included in those meetings.

Ben made the rounds that morning, stopping as usual by Elliott's room first. "What's the latest on the mega-cane?" Elliott told him he hadn't finished downloading all the data, but it appeared the storm had increased its forward speed during the night. "That is the good news because it might come and go over us before the blizzard hits. We could deal with them easier as two events rather than one combined. The bad news is that the hurricane has increased in intensity

... the eye wall is now registering 160 MPH winds ... none of this makes any scientific sense Ben, because making landfall always reduces the wind speed."

Seeing the frustrated look on Ben's face, Elliott said "I can't do a damn thing to stop or divert the storm Ben ... I can only tell you what I see ... and it isn't good. The rain started before breakfast and by nightfall we will definitely feel effects of high winds. Tomorrow and the next day will be the real test." Ben said he wanted to check with Ethan and make sure all the equipment was running well with no glitches. Elliott stared at the empty doorway after Ben left and with a jolt realized that of all the people on the team, Ben was probably the weakest link at this point. He had had a gifted life and most of his years were spent in philanthropic work. His crowning success was developing and partially financing the compound project. He knew then that Ben had not given a lot of consideration to walking this walk. This would be the biggest test he had ever been through.

The concept had been brilliant, Elliott thought, but it wasn't without its flaws. Some of the team worked full days without let up like Genevieve and Fawn in the kitchen, the housekeeping team ... others worked on an 'on call' basis like Polly the hairdresser, Joshua and Janice who were the medical team, and Samuel the Chaplain. The security team had a rotating shift. Margaret was able to leave her work room once her record keeping and reporting was finished. Winston and Ethan were in constant alert mode monitoring the equipment which made the house liveable. He kept regular hours in his work room, and it was all he could do to keep up with all the monitors and the communications network. Now that the compound was fully occupied and functioning, Ben didn't have a real job to do except to see to it that everyone else did theirs. Elliott hoped that Ben would be able to see this through and live up to his role as 'leader'. Time would tell and it wouldn't be a long time away.

That evening in the gathering room all eyes were on Elliott and he knew what everyone wanted to hear about. "We all know what a hurricane is and some of us have been through one. Trouble is, none of us has been exposed to one like we are facing now. The last report I had showed the forward movement had stabilized and the winds were exceeding 160 MPH. This means we will be exposed to this storm's strongest fury for a longer time than earlier thought. Tonight the rain will increase significantly, as well as the wind. Tomorrow and the next day we will be in full hurricane mode. Our house ... and our courage will be tested ... maybe not to the limit but close to it. We should all try to follow our standard routine as closely as we can.

"If there is any good news to report it is that the blizzard coming at us from the west has slowed its forward movement but it is dropping beyond record setting depths of snow in the mid west. Our communication with the Iowa compound has not been compromised by the snowstorm, and they report they are fully functional at this point, although totally isolated from the rest of the world they can see. Most of their view of houses and other buildings have become a solid blanket of white with an occasional red silo pointing through the blanket. We are hoping the hurricane ... at least most of it ... will have passed by the time the blizzard hits us." Elliott didn't mention that the Yellowstone volcano continued on its upward climb of seismic activity. No point in borrowing trouble unless he had to.

Margaret collected verbal reports from everyone else and that was the end of the meeting. Some decided to go to their living quarters; others to the gym; others lingered over the coffee and pastries Genevieve had put out. Elliott went to the gym to work off some of his adrenaline and Margaret stayed to play cards.

CHAPTER 46

Elliott and Margaret were awakened early the next morning by the sound of a loud crash. Jumping up the see what had literally befallen them, they rushed to the gathering room where the sound had come from. Several others were already there and they all stared at a huge tree leaning against the convex LAMEX window. Part of the top had broken away in the fall and the jagged trunk had hit the house where it still rested. Through early light they could see the trees outside being whipped around like they were on the spin cycle of some giant washing machine. Pelting rain was coming at the house sideways, hitting the same window head on.

When Ben came into the gathering room moments later and saw the perilous situation, he called Ethan in immediately to assess the situation. "Ethan, what exactly are the specs for this LAMEX window?"

Ethan ran back to his work room to gather the architectural prints. He laid them out on the dining table and after examining all the scientific data he said "the material itself can withstand wind speeds of 100 MPH, and the convex structure adds to that durability. I don't think it occurred to anyone to test the weight of a half ton tree falling against it".

Knowing the safety of the entire house depended on this wall holding together, Ben asked Ethan for his best assessment. "The fact that it didn't penetrate the structure when it first fell, and is still leaning at an angle, I suspect it will hold unless something else adds weight to it such as snow, or the winds get so high the trunk actually moves. Being a jagged edge, all the weight is focused on a small portion of the trunk."

Ben pressed him for a solution. "We can use haz-mat suits ... I and three other men could go outside and cut the trunk of the tree with the chain saws from the underground bunker. The first thing I want to do is go down to the second floor and see if that window suffered any damage."

By then everyone in the house had come to the dining room. Ben spoke up, "good idea Ethan ... I'll go, Winston you come and Drake too. Elliott, check the monitors in your work room and get any information you can about the storm. Genevieve, you and Fawn set up the table in the gathering room for breakfast. The dining room is now off limits to everyone except those of us working on the situation. If this window breaks, I don't have to tell you what will happen then."

Margaret and Polly quickly rearranged the furniture in the gathering room so that most everyone had a chair at the table for the first sitting; hopefully the second shift of the four men could take their place. Genevieve and Fawn brought in bowls of food to be passed family style. Samuel took Ben's place at the head of the table and automatically everyone bowed their head for his prayer of thanksgiving and asking God to spare them and keep them safe. Everyone said 'amen' in unison without even thinking about it. They ate in silence although by then the howl of the winds and trees brushing against the house was loud enough to drown out any conversation ... even there in the inner core of the house.

Samuel tried to add a touch of levity to the obvious by saying in a loud voice, "perhaps next time they will make these places sound proof as well as bullet proof ... if there is a next time". Everyone nodded or smiled at Samuel, not wanting his attempt at calm falling on deaf ears.

When Elliott came into the gathering room, everyone stopped eating and looked at him for information. "NOAA is reporting mass casualties from the hurricane, but still no numbers or dollar amounts on Florida's damage. The storm is now covering the entire state of Georgia and FEMA has offered a grim outcome for the folks evacuated to the eastern part of the state. Of course that knowledge is for our ears only and not being broadcast over the Emergency Broadcast channel. We are now under the northern bands of the storm and as the day passes, the intensity will increase. Our wind gauge is at 70 MPH sustained winds, with gusts to 100."

Elliott had opened the whole house intercom so the men on the floor below them could hear his report. Ben, Ethan, Winston and Drake had found no damage to the lower floor or the window, but hearing Elliott's forecast, they made an immediate decision to rush through the tunnel and retrieve the chainsaws from the bunker to cut the 12" jagged tree trunk leaning against the upstairs window. The four then donned a Kevlar vest and a haz-mat suit to protect themselves from the storm. Before going outside the basement they formulated a plan as to who would do what in the quickest way possible.

They made their way out of the small passage door and each began their own task, chainsaw in hand. They were to each cut a section at the same time, letting the four foot sections drop in tandem. Winston was making the cut closest to the ground and when Drake's next section fell, it flipped out and caught Winston, pinning him to the ground by his left arm. The remaining trunk fell away from the window and the men. Immediately the three dropped their saws and began to lift the four foot section of twelve inch trunk from Winston's arm. It was mangled and blood was coming through the haz-mat suit where it had been ripped open.

Their goggles were of little protection against the elements since it was all the three could do to stand. By instinct Drake grabbed two branches from the ground and put them on either side of Winston's arm ... ripping some vine from its roots to wind around the makeshift splint to hold it in place. They couldn't speak for the roar of the storm, so Ben motioned to Drake and Ethan to carry Winston and he would open the door. Once inside, Ben called Joshua and told him and Janice to be prepared to treat Winston's injury. The three ... and the wounded being carried ... made their way back to the top floor ... still in their goggles and haz-mat suits, sopping wet.

BLACK SNOW ... by Anne Rushton

Joshua and Janice had moved into crisis mode ... something not unfamiliar to either of them. Once they rested Winston on the medical table in Joshua's work room, the other three left to give him and Janice room to work.

Being barred from the dining room, the others in the house had not seen what happened ... only heard the thud of the tree trunk as it hit the ground. They felt safe in returning to the dining room once Samuel peeked in and gave the 'all clear' signal. What they did see was three exhausted men in haz-mat gear rush a bleeding Winston through to Joshua's work room. Ben, Ethan and Drake reappeared, taking off their headgear and stopping long enough to give the others an update of what had happened. Ben said "mission accomplished; one casualty of unknown injury. Joshua and Janice are working on Winston now".

CHAPTER 47

After the three men had returned to the basement, Drake volunteered to retrieve the chainsaws they had left outside. The other two men opened the door just enough for him to go out and then lean their combined weight against it to get it closed. Drake virtually crawled to the chainsaws and got back to the opened door as fast as he could. They left the saws by the door in case they were needed again. With the hanging haz-mat suits left to dry, Ethan, Drake and Ben returned to the dining room to a cheering group. They had indeed saved the day ... and perhaps the rest of all their lives. There was no word on Winston's condition yet, so they all returned to the gathering room to finish the meal. The food was cold, the coffee was being reheated, but it was one of the best meals any of them had ever eaten.

Ben passed out wireless earphones so they could communicate over the storm, leaving three at Joshua's door. As Janice came out a few minutes later, she saw the earphones and immediately put a set on and spoke to the gathered group. "Winston has lost a lot of blood and will need some from one of you. Is anyone a universal donor with Type O blood?" Jamison volunteered to be the donor and went back to what by then had become a surgical suite. There was no time for formalities, so Janice set up a donor to recipient line while Joshua continued the surgery.

With the tree crisis over, Ben encouraged everyone to re-establish a semblance of routine amid the howling storm

BLACK SNOW ... by Anne Rushton

... there was nothing to be gained by just sitting and waiting on news about Winston ... or waiting for the next crisis. There was work to be done. Elliott returned to his monitoring station, Margaret began her reporting for the day, Claudia and her team restored order to the dining room and gathering room once Genevieve and Fawn had cleared the remnants of breakfast from the table.

Ethan monitored all the house's systems then went downstairs to make a visual inspection. Polly began working the adrenaline from Ben's shoulders, then Drake, then Ethan when he finished his rounds. Leah was pulling her shift in security monitoring; Samuel made the rounds, giving words of encouragement where needed. For the first time every member of the compound was either working at top speed or in what had become a makeshift surgical suite. Ben was humbled at the efficiency of the group he had brought together and in somewhat of an epiphany, realized he was only the vessel through which the water was poured. He had been the idea man, the money man ... now the group was keeping the group together and safe ... so far.

Genevieve sent around a message that there would be a snack lunch buffet in the dining room and a full dinner at 6. Joshua announced through the headphone system that Winston's surgery was complete. He said Winston would remain in his work-room-turned-surgical-suite throughout the day and night. He and Janice would rotate in observation. He waited until the end-of-day gathering to report the details of

Winston's injuries.

During the remainder of the day the most tedious detail to deal with was the continuous onslaught of increasing wind and rain. Branches from the acres of trees pelted the front curved window ... and every other window. Though they were all made of bullet proof glass, Ben voiced concern about them shattering just from the wind velocity which by late afternoon had reached a steady 120 MPH with gusts over 150. The decision was made to lower all the interior steel shades over the windows ... all except for one section in the dining room. This put more of a strain on the lighting system for the house and more of a strain on already frayed nerves ... Samuel knew about the psychological affect of being in confined quarters without seeing daylight.

In the gathering room after dinner they all spoke and listened over their earphones. Even though the winds continued to increase, they had been muffled by the steel shades. Ben asked Joshua to go first since they were all so anxious to learn about Winston. "The most important thing is that he will survive. The tree trunk crushed the bone, muscle tissue, arteries, veins, ligaments and tendons in his lower left arm and hand. Even in a first class hospital setting, there would have been no option but to amputate below his elbow which I did. Janice is with him now. He has overcome the anesthesia, but I am keeping him sedated for pain control ... at least for another twenty-four hours. Jamison donated about two pints of blood to Winston during the surgery, all the time being exposed to the obviously gruesome injury Winston sustained and what I had to do to make it right. We have adequate IV solutions to sustain him nutritionally and keep him hydrated for another week, which I don't think will be needed. He should be awake by day after tomorrow and alert and taking nourishment by mouth later that day. By then he will need Samuel's help as much as mine or Janice's."

CHAPTER 48

Ben explained how they had resolved the fallen tree problem earlier that day and the details of how Winston was hurt. Ethan reported on his examination of the convex windows on both the upper and lower floor and pronounced them sound, in spite of the tree and added "we have dodged our first bullet". He reminded the group the house was operating on energy from the fuel cells ... generated, for the most part, from captured sunlight. With the steel shades nearly closed in the dining room and fully closed on the floor below them, their source of energy was blocked. They should be fine for about a week, but longer than that and electricity would be rotated among the zones of the house. Heating water would be eliminated during the night hours and heating the house would be reduced during that time as well.

Elliott gave his dismal forecast "continuous and increasing rain and wind throughout the night into tomorrow. At some point during the afternoon tomorrow we will have our biggest test when the edge of the eye wall of the hurricane passes overhead ... wind and rain will max out at that point. For safety, I am suggesting that anyone who is not doing some work come to this center core room. There is still a great danger of tornadoes being spun off from the storm and there will be a period of time during the apex of the hurricane when we may not be able to distinguish between the hurricane and a tornado ... the force will be that great. Ben, I suggest you close the steel shade completely in the dining room tonight. We don't really know what to expect in terms of wind velocity. All the gauges in the storm's path have been maxed out. As most of you know, once the eye wall passes over, there will be a period of eerie calm with clear skies and sunlight. This won't last long since the center of circulation has tightened to the point of nearly being invisible from satellite detection. The other side of the storm will then start to pass over with the same maximum force and will diminish as the hours pass. We might see some relief the following day, but it won't just go away ... it will taper off throughout the coming week".

Housekeeping assistant Amber spoke up "can we all go home then?"

Elliott responded to her question as well as telling the group "we have another threat coming in from the west that could make the hurricane seem like an afternoon rain. An enormous blizzard which will reach us by next week ... it has already dropped snow measured in feet and drifts being measured in double digits in places. All the midwestern states have been placed in a state of emergency with martial law imposed by the President. Anyone crazy enough to expose themselves to pelting ice and snow and below freezing temperatures will die within minutes outside. The winds alone can freeze you from the inside out when you breathe. I'll have more on the blizzard later ... for now let's get through the hurricane".

BLACK SNOW ... by Anne Rushton

Margaret was taking notes from everyone at a furious pace to put in her reports tomorrow morning. Ben nodded to Samuel who asked anyone who wanted to join him in prayer to do so. All heads bowed. Everyone in the room had by then wanted all the help they could get. Even if they had never prayed before, they did then. It was their turn to be 'in the foxhole with bullets flying overhead'.

CHAPTER 49

Elliott went back to his work room where he was prepared to stay as long as he could stay awake. Genevieve brought him a thermos of coffee and some sugary snacks to help. Ben dropped by after he had closed the steel shades in the dining room and offered to relieve Elliott for part of the night. Elliott accepted and said he would call him when he could work no longer. Jamison was right behind Ben with the same offer and Elliott nodded in appreciation. He couldn't recall a situation in his life when he felt more needed, more part of a team, more endangered or more bonded to a group of people who were giving everything they had to the common cause.

The compound had been activated for ... how long now ... a week ... a few days. Elliott was dazed by the thought that he hadn't been keeping track. He could see the date on his various monitors, but he realized some of the psychological effects of being a POW were some of the things the group would ... or already had ... endured ... without the abuse. Shuttered away from 'normal', not seeing the sun, always being in high alert or crisis mode, the unpredictable future, not knowing if ... or when ... any of them would be 'released'. Yet, they all came voluntarily, he reminded himself ... but could anyone have dreamed of what they had signed up for. The storm and the storm to come ...

Elliott was startled out of his introspection by the sound of an alarm on one of his monitors which meant a major bulletin was coming up on the Emergency Broadcast System.

"The President has suspended operation of all stock exchanges east of the Mississippi River. All banks under the FDIC umbrella east of the Mississippi River will be closed immediately and not re-open until further notice. ATM machines will dispense $100 per account during each 24 hour period to meet immediate needs. The postal system east of the Mississippi River will be closed effective immediately until further notice. All mail will be held until it is safe for delivery. This includes, but is not limited to, all first class mail, bulk mail, express mail and parcels. All outbound plane service has been suspended effective immediately east of the Mississippi River and all airports will close tomorrow morning at 8:00 A.M. to allow inbound flights to land. Bus, train, monorail service is likewise suspended effective immediately east of the Mississippi River.

"Everyone east of the Mississippi River, excluding hospitals, nursing homes, assisted living facilities and prisons are ordered to evacuate and seek shelter in one of the designated shelters streaming across the bottom of your screen. All schools are closed immediately and those deemed serviceable will serve as emergency shelters. Those in the above listed categories who are not ordered to seek shelter are ordered to shelter in place, consolidate patients and/or inmates as much as is possible and to be ready for loss of power perhaps for more than a week. All Federal and

BLACK SNOW ... by Anne Rushton

State workers are ordered to stay at home, including persons associated with the Court systems under Federal, State and County jurisdiction."

"First responders should shelter in place and if able, respond to emergency calls only. The interstate highway system east of the Mississippi River is now closed and motorists must leave by the closest exit and seek shelter. State and County Road Departments are at liberty to decide the advisability of activating emergency road maintenance for the purposes of plowing, salting, establishing detours, closing hazardous roads during inclement weather."

Elliott wondered what he had missed ... had he fallen asleep ... why were these restrictions being put into place now ... one look at the updated NOAA weather map answered his questions.

"Holy Mother of God" he whispered to himself. Invoking a long forgotten Catholic tradition, he crossed himself.

CHAPTER 50

Ben had come into Elliott's work room to relieve him and heard his comment. "Translate that for me Elliott."

Elliott pointed to the weather map monitor and Ben just stared in disbelief. The blizzard had grown to a monstrous size ... reaching from Canada on the north to mid-Texas on the south. The leading edge was less than a hundred miles west of the Mississippi River. "What happened Elliott?"

"Ben, I think we can just toss out all the books ever written about weather and what happens when certain conditions are created. This is so totally beyond my understanding and from what I hear, everyone ... including NOAA ... has ceased making predictions of any kind. To answer your question, 'I wish the Hell I knew' ... you likely know as much now as I do and all I can do is see total disaster in the making."

Ben sat down to watch and Elliott began checking in with the other compounds affected ... communication was either non existent or intermittent. The blizzard was wiping out even the most sophisticated communications technology. "I can't make connections with the compound west of St. Louis which could mean either they have lost their satellite uplink ... or worst case scenario, the compound could have failed altogether for any number of reasons. The blizzard's forward movement has reached a speed where it will reach us either as soon as the hurricane moves out or overlap the tail end of it."

BLACK SNOW ... by Anne Rushton

"Elliott, I want you to get some rest ... the group can't afford for you to go under from stress ... you look awful and all that coffee has given you the jitters ... add to that the storms and ... anyway, I am relieving you of your command for at least eight hours. I am going to call Joshua and have him give you a mild sedative."

When Elliott tried to stand, he was lightheaded and knew if he didn't sit down, he would fall. He heard Ben call Joshua and within a couple of minutes Joshua was at Elliott's work room. Joshua told him to go to bed and he would quietly slip in and give him the injection. If Margaret woke up, he would think of something to tell her. With Ben's help, he made it to bed, let his clothes fall to the floor and laid down. His body was actually asleep before the sedative was given.

Joshua slipped out past a sleeping Margaret and returned to the work room that Ben was now commanding. "He's out like a light and won't wake up for about six hours ... eight if we are lucky. Ben, what is going on?"

"What is going on ... do you mean technically? If so, then I don't have a clue and I don't think Elliott does either. He has worked himself into such a state because most of the knowledge he has accumulated right now is just like so much snow. Mother Nature has rewritten the rule book ... or the weather code ... I know it has something to do with global warming, but take a look at that weather monitor and tell me what you see."

BLACK SNOW ... by Anne Rushton

"Is all that white area the blizzard Elliott has been warning us about?"

"Yep ... and not only that but tonight the President has pretty much ordered a lock down of everything east of the Mississippi River ... here, I printed the bulletin ... read it for yourself."

"Before he collapsed Elliott told me he suspected we have lost the compound west of St. Louis ... and just before you came back in, I saw the connection light with Tulsa's compound turn from green to red. The blizzard must have taken it out or they have lost contact with the world beyond their compound. I have no idea if or when we will get a real status update of the compounds we now can't reach."

"If I am reading this right Ben, the light just went out for the Shreveport compound as well. Ben, what can we do ... or should do ... anything different than what we are doing now which is to just sit here and wait? We had a damn near close call with that tree thing."

"Joshua it is like trying to count the grains of sand before the next wave comes over the beach and takes some of them back out to sea. We have to take each hour at a time ... and deal with whatever crisis comes up. You know, the compound project is an experiment ... never been tried before now ... and that is one reason you do an experiment ... to see if will work the way you think it will. The best minds put this thing together, hoping it would work during a worst case scenario. I think this is going to be just that ... and God help us all if what we have done still isn't enough to survive. Maybe nature truly is reclaiming this part of the world and starting over ... you know, wiping the slate clean for a 'do over' since we have made such a crappy mess of things."

By then, it was daylight ... or at least when daylight should first appear. Except for a sliver through the front window where they could take a visual look at the destruction the hurricane was leaving in its wake, they only had monitors to tell them how bad it was. Like putting a plane on auto-pilot in dense fog ... hoping it would fly right and checking the monitors to see what was out there.

Most everyone was up except for Elliott and Winston. Ear plugs replaced their headphones for sleeping so they wouldn't be kept awake by the roar and howl and sound of trees snapping or brushing against the house. What the compound didn't need then was a group of people dead on their feet from lack of rest.

CHAPTER 51

Joshua couldn't afford the luxury of a sedative ... he had to be alert, so he went back to his bedroom to rest, knowing he wouldn't get any more sleep that night. Janice had been with Winston during the night. Just as Joshua was beginning to relax in the bed, she came in to give him an update on Winston and together they decided to let him wake up naturally that afternoon. He would need pain medication, but he was part of the team and might need to advise Ethan about monitoring the water systems.

"Joshua, you know all my nursing experience has been in trauma ... we either patch them up enough to go to surgery or ICU, or to the morgue. I never saw the patients after they left the emergency room. I hope your experience as a doctor will give you the right words when it comes time to tell Winston what happened ... I mean about losing his arm."

"Don't worry, I'll take care of that."

They heard the call to breakfast and saw everyone there except for Ben, Winston and of course, Elliott. Joshua checked on him on the way and he was still in a deep sleep. Winston was likewise. On the way to the dining room they passed Fawn who was taking a plate of food and coffee to Ben in Elliott's work room and to whoever was in security.

The first thing everyone did when they came to the dining room was go look out the window. Daylight was trying to push its way through the clouds and rain with little success. All they could see were a few trees left standing with branches and tree trunks strewn everywhere like just so many huge matchsticks broken and twisted into hideous shapes.

Amber, one of Claudia's assistants, was the first to say anything after they had served themselves and were sitting at the table. "I remember when I first came here ... there was so much wildlife ... squirrels, deer, rabbits, foxes, mountain cats, birds. I wonder where they are now."

Samuel said "you know, animals have such a superior connection to nature beyond what man's is. They know somehow when something like this is about to happen and they make provisions, just like we have here. They eat heavier for days and when the time comes, they go underground to their dens or caves or burrows to wait it out ... at least I hope they have. I think God endowed them with a special ability to be prepared. We as humans have become what we consider to be 'so far advanced' over the other animals. Truth is, when something like this happens, we are at the mercy of whatever happens. We have lost that innate ability to sense trouble. We have to be told to run for cover."

Janice updated the group on Winston's condition. "Joshua has stopped giving him sedation and we are hoping he will wake up on his own this afternoon. Of course we will keep him on pain killers. To answer your unasked question, Joshua is going to tell him about his arm ... although unless one of us is with him, he will be aware of the pain and likely will feel for himself what happened. It's different being a trauma nurse in a room full of co-workers doing your part on an unknown person ... it's another thing to have something like this happen to a friend. He will need a substantial period of adjustment, but we need his mind and knowledge to keep the water resources working. He will have to teach Ethan what he doesn't know already and just be an advisor for the time being."

They were all back to wearing the headphones to communicate because of the sounds coming from outside. A quick look outside the window told them what the devastating hurricane had done to the landscape within their limited view, and they could only speculate what Atlanta and other cities in its path must look like. Ben had often cautioned them not to dwell on the storm because they had taken every precaution they could ... and not to speculate on what it was doing elsewhere. Thoughts like that need to be forced out of your mind ... at the least they were distracting them from their work ... and at the worst, it could cause a mental breakdown ... something none of them could afford. They carried on in conversation and their duties keeping those thoughts foremost in their mind. Still ... it couldn't be forgotten ... the noise and wind and pelting sheets of rain were relentless.

Ben came to the dining room for a coffee refill and sat down briefly to give them all an update. "For the time being I am in the command center ... Elliott's work room. Last night he worked to the point of exhaustion and Joshua gave him some light sedation to force him into sleeping. Sit down Margaret ... he is fine ... you don't need to charge in there to check on him ... I just did. We need to have him fresh when he wakes up.

"I wanted to let you know we have another development, like we need more problems to deal with. Without going into all the details, the blizzard has expanded to the point there is no way we can miss getting hit by its full force and fury. If we are lucky, the hurricane will be gone or almost gone by the time it hits us. We are still in direct communication with FEMA, DHS and the White House.

"At this point there is nothing the agencies can do. They will shelter in place and the White House will keep the line of communication open from their bunker. We have lost touch with several of the compounds and at this point, it would only be a guess why. Remember my cautioning you about speculation. Once the eye wall passes over some time today we will have a period of calm and daylight followed by the other side of the hurricane. Once that occurs, we can look forward to having been through the worst of it since the winds and rain will slowly diminish over time.

"The good news is that there is little likelihood anyone would be out in this looking to do us harm. For one thing, no one could even stand up outside, and the only vehicles running are military combat type vehicles. We won't see any cars for a long time ... Drake tells me the night vision cameras revealed that our road was washed away hours ago. So far the house has not suffered any kind of significant damage."

"Claudia, where is Amber?"

"When I didn't see her in here, I assumed she was in the bathroom ... I'll go check on her."

In a few minutes, Claudia came rushing back. "I can't find her anywhere on this floor or in the pantry below ... ".

"Does she ever go to the gym" Ben asked Claudia. "I have never known her to do that."

"OK, Drake check the basement ... cars, weapons room. I'll check the only other place she could be. Leah come with me."

Quietly, Ben and Leah descended the staircase down to the basement. Ben used his magnetic key to open the door to the small elevator room and put out his arm to stop Leah from moving into it. "Shhh" he put his finger to his lips and whispered to Leah that he heard faint crying.

Making their way into the tunnel leading to the bunker, they both put their weapons away. The light from the elevator room cast an eery glow on the tunnel. Leah called out softly, "Amber ... hon, what are you doing down here?"

Having been discovered, Amber began to sob loudly and uncontrollably. Neither Ben nor Leah could make sense of anything she was saying, although they caught a few words ... 'sun' ... 'gone' ... 'snow' ... 'shutter'... 'the bunnies'.

BLACK SNOW ... by Anne Rushton

Ben and Leah advanced quickly to find Amber sitting in a fetal position rocking back and forth aimlessly. Leah whispered to Ben to go get Joshua and Samuel ... "tell Joshua to bring a sedative ... I'll stay here. Don't worry, I have defended myself against a much bigger foe than this helpless child. Ben, I am a Marine ... remember ... SIR?" Ben nodded and once Leah settled down to hold Amber in a motherly embrace, he left. Taking two stairs at a time, he quickly summoned Joshua and Samuel. Within what seemed only a minute, the three returned to find Amber in Leah's arms limp, but whimpering. Joshua soon had her sedated and being twice Amber's size, Leah carried her easily to the elevator which took them to the main floor.

The running and commotion had alerted everyone and they all waited in the dining room.

Ben spoke up as Joshua and Samuel carried Amber to Janice's office. "I suppose it was too much to ask that everyone come through this nightmare unscathed emotionally. Was Amber the one to ask the other night if we could all go home after the storm ... or was it someone else ... never mind. I remember earlier her talking about the wildlife and Samuel trying to soothe her sad thoughts. I guess it was just all too much weight for her to carry on those small shoulders. No, I don't know how she got to the tunnel. We all have a breaking point ... perhaps it was asking too much of her ... of anyone ... to come here."

CHAPTER 52

Elliott dragged himself out of bed in late afternoon in time to hear noise come from the dining room. He threw on a robe and rushed in to see the group gathered at the unshuttered full width window. She sun was out, the winds were still and the rain had slowed to a drizzle. It took some time for their ears to adjust to the silence. It took their mind longer to wrap around the devastation they saw in all directions. Only a few of the trees were left standing in what only a few days before had been a beautiful evergreen forest ... and the ones left were stripped bare of their needles. What had once been the road at the foot of the hill was now a raging river. A lake in the distance had once been farmland. Splinters of wood and roofing ... mixed with furniture parts and parts they didn't want to think about ... were scattered between them and the horizon. There wasn't a hint of life anywhere.

"We are an island unto ourselves aren't we Ben?"

"For now Jamison ... but we are still here ... and I for one want to thank Ethan for designing and building a structure that has kept us at a distance from disaster." One by one they gathered around Ethan and shook hands or gave him a hug. No words were spoken ... none were necessary.

Margaret and Elliott found each other in the group and hugged tightly. Ben asked Elliott how he was feeling. "Much better thank you, and thanks to Joshua my own batteries are recharged and I am ready to relieve you in the command center." Ben nodded and gave Elliott a look up and down and Elliott realized he was still standing there half exposed in his short robe. Never missing a chance to bring levity to any situation, Genevieve said in an exaggerated French accent "Elliott, be a good boy now and go put your pants on ... I'll see if I can find you a morsel left from lunch".

Janice had stayed in her office with a sedated Amber, and Joshua had stayed with Winston during the brief sun celebration ... the noise must have pushed him into consciousness. Janice joined the two and they waited until Winston was fully awake and began asking questions. At first Winston just looked around and muttered 'Joshua' and 'Janice' ... looking at each one with a question mark after speaking each name. Joshua decided the sooner they got this over the better. "Winston, do you know where you are?"

Winston looked around and said "the house".

"Do you remember what happened to you?"

Winston nodded ... and then felt for his left arm. He let out a muffled scream and then began to sob uncontrollably. "Winston, I had to do that to save your life ... I had no choice ... even if we had been in the best hospital in the country, the outcome would have been the same. I know what I tell you is of little consolation, but you did survive, and in time, can be fitted with a bionic prosthesis which will allow you to do almost everything you did before. Advances in recent years have been wonderful ... they will attach your nerve endings and you will be able to 'feel' your fingers and lower arm.

BLACK SNOW ... by Anne Rushton

"Winston I hope in time you can appreciate the fact that you helped save the house and everyone here ... and now we need your help again. I know the pain is terrible and I promise to help you with that, but we need your knowledge of our water system."

"How long ..." Winston muttered.

"This happened a couple days ago ... to tell you the truth we are all having a hard time keeping track of time. Janice helped me patch you up ... you had lost a lot of blood by the time they got you here ... Jamison sat in that chair to your right and we infused you with his Type O blood directly."

"I'm lucky I didn't get killed. I just need some time to adjust and some of your pain meds. You know I am here for the long haul and this could have happened to anyone."

"... and may still" Joshua added. "We have been through a lot so far with the hurricane and the eye wall is just now passing over so we have half of it yet to endure. If that wasn't bad enough, there is a massive blizzard headed our way out of the west. I will have Elliott fill you in later. Do you think you could sit up and dangle your feet over the bed?"

With Joshua and Janice's help, he got to a sitting position and swivelled around to slide his legs over the edge of the bed. "Good going ... how do you feel?"

"A little dizzy Janice, but at least in time I can walk on two good legs. Could I try to sit in that chair for a few minutes ... I really want to get back to the living. Being here in the compound is a challenge enough without my absence." They helped him stand and told him to stare straight ahead and focus on something ... not to look down. Winston steadied himself and slowly inched to the chair. He smiled when he saw Joshua and Janice's excitement that he had made such progress.

Having fully waked up, Winston was suddenly overcome with hysterical sobbing. "Janice, I can feel my arm ... and my left hand ... but it's gone ... oh my God, how can I live with this" he said amid the tears and pain. "I am useless now and I will never be a whole person again."

"Winston, what you feel is real ... it's called 'phantom appendage pain' and you will likely experience that for some time. It has to do with the nerve endings in your upper arm adjusting to the loss. Try not to be further traumatized by it." Janice bent over and held his head against her chest in a gesture of comfort, all the while feeling Winston's body shake from the pain and fear and anger and all the other emotions someone in his situation feels.

Trying to pull himself together Winston said "what's all the commotion about Joshua ... I hear laughing."

"The group is happy to see the sun. Ben had pulled the steel shutters down in everyone's room, as well as the window wall in the dining room. He opened it back up to gather some of the sun's energy while we are 'inside the eye wall of the hurricane'."

Still trying to regain his composure Winston said "seems I have missed a lot ... you don't by chance have a wheelchair do you?"

Joshua held up the palm of his hand, went into Janice's adjoining office, came back in pushing a wheelchair and asked Winston if he felt up to a ride. "You bet ... I want to see the sun too."

When Winston was pushed into the dining room everyone gave a loud cheer to see him. They truly were a family by then and one of their own had rejoined them. "Thanks everyone ... I still want to be part of the team. I just need some time ... for now, I can direct Ethan from the sidelines. Before breaking into sobs again, he muttered "thanks for caring about me".

As the group surrounded Winston in support, a cloud blocked the sun's rays and it began to rain again.

CHAPTER 53

Ben asked Ethan to close the window wall all of the way across, as it had been during the worst of the hurricane and to do the same on the floor below them. As Ben watched the group mourn the loss of daylight, he said "we are in the storm again, but our batteries got charged by more than the sun with Winston 'coming home'. Now lets get back to work."

When Joshua pushed Winston past Elliott's room, he wanted to stop and get a detailed update. Elliott said "come in ... I am more than happy to see you ... I will push him back to your room in a few minutes Joshua."

Some time later, Genevieve had Elliott announce dinner and they gathered as usual ... this time someone pushing Winston directly to his place at the table. Samuel offered his by then standard prayer of thanksgiving and prayer for safety. This time he added an appeal for Amber and for Winston's continued healing.

"What happened to Amber?" Winston asked. Ben said she had gone missing earlier in the day and they would talk about it after dinner.

Earlier everyone had gone back to wearing earphones and someone put a set on Winston. Genevieve brought Winston a light meal of broth and crackers, hoping it would be a good first meal after several days of a forced fast, except for the IV.

BLACK SNOW ... by Anne Rushton

After everyone ate, they moved to the gathering room. Ben's first order of business was to officially welcome Winston back to the team and extend a collective heartfelt sadness at what had happened to him. Ben also spoke for the group when he commended Winston's courage and bravery ... and expressed sincere appreciation for Winston's role in perhaps saving the entire project ... certainly the house. Ben then asked Joshua and Samuel to update the group on Amber's status.

"Samuel and I have conferred and feel that Amber must be relieved of her duties ... at least for the time being. She has suffered some sort of disconnect with reality and appears to have been catapulted into a clinical ... or circumstantial ... depression. The enormity of the suffering ... not for herself, but for all living things ... for people, livestock and other creatures ... was more than she could cope with. As a defense mechanism, she has disconnected with reality. She keeps calling them 'the innocents'.

"She isn't a danger to herself or others ... just the opposite. Her level of caring was too significant to have made her a good candidate for this project. No one is to blame for this ... least of all you Claudia for having chosen her. We never considered disqualifying someone because they had an overabundance of compassion. She will likely remain in the state she is in indefinitely and will become one of the casualties as surely as if she had been buried in a snowdrift."

Samuel spoke up "if I might, I would like to add ... wearing my psychologist's hat at this point, that this is exactly what Ben has warned us about. As hard as it is, we must focus on our work and let it be our total distraction."

Ben asked, "what plan have you two fashioned for Amber's care?"

Joshua suggested keeping her on a very low maintenance dose of sedative for the foreseeable future. The dosage would allow her to interact with the others. Any time anyone has the time they could supervise her in the gathering room so that she would have access to books and music. Samuel added, "at best it is a patchwork quilt and not what we would like for her ... but under the circumstances, it's all we can provide. I will become her direct support person ... perhaps she can view me in a father role. She will come to trust me as her 'go to' person, freeing the rest of you to carry out your work. Speaking of which I'm sure Claudia and Jo would appreciate any help any of us can give them with the laundry or cleaning in Fawn's absence."

Ben was silent longer than usual and without looking up, he asked Elliott for a weather update.

CHAPTER 54

"Glad you didn't ask for a weather 'forecast' Ben ... I think that word will soon be taken from the dictionary and disappear from disuse. We are now under the southern side of the hurricane as you can hear ... even with the earphones on. The sound is much worse than before ... without our forest to muffle some of it's roar. The good news is that it will, over time, diminish and I am encouraged to think we will all survive ... physically. Ben, you and Ethan are to be commended for putting together such a magnificent structure here to endure what it has been thru." Ben and Ethan made a gesture of tipping their hats.

"As you know by now, even though we are literally 'out of the woods' caused by the hurricane, we are by no means out of the woods figuratively speaking. I think the hurricane would be considered a warm up for the main event ... the blizzard heading our way. Before it's over, it will have blanketed half the country north to south. We expect the hurricane to be out of here by midday tomorrow and sometime tomorrow morning we will start to see snow flurries.

"I know textbooks teach us that hurricanes are driven by warm air; snow blizzards are driven by cold air. We can toss the textbooks ... I think if we ever use them again, they will have to be re-written. Something is going on in the atmosphere that we don't understand. My best guess is global warming and climate change has taken place in significant ways ... ways we can't begin to understand now.

229

BLACK SNOW ... by Anne Rushton

We are in new territory and mostly it is just wait-and-see."

Ben asked "what are the wind factors and snowfall totals elsewhere".

Elliott looked down and took a deep breath before he could bring himself to let the group in on what he knew from FEMA and the few other compounds he was still in touch with. "Wind speeds will be nearly those of a Category 4 hurricane. Snow totals will likely be measured in feet rather than inches, and drifts in sheltered areas could reach ten or more feet". There was an audible gasp from the group as they sat spellbound listening to Elliott deliver what some considered a death sentence.

As Elliott said it would, the winds began to diminish little by little throughout the afternoon. He knew that was small comfort to anyone. He surmised some of them once thought that after the hurricane passed the worst was over and they would get a dusting of snow. With any luck, roads would start to be repaired by the National Guard and FEMA, and they could all pack up and go home ... if they still had a home to go to. Elliott knew he had dashed all their hopes of that happening. Still, they had to know what to expect.

By night fall, earphones were removed and the steel shades had been withdrawn in all the rooms. Even in the dark, all they could see outside was what looked like a war zone. In some way it had been a war ... waged by nature against its human enemy. In the process it was destroying some of its own creation.

BLACK SNOW ... by Anne Rushton

Elliott was jolted from his reverie by one of the green compound lights turning from green to red. He immediately tried to contact the Arkansas compound but there was no response. Here again, there was no way of knowing if communications were just compromised by the storm, or if the compound had failed. By then, half of his ten monitoring lights ... one for each compound including Jardin ... were red. That left them, 'Compound 1', and four others still communicating. The others were all located along the eastern seaboard and it literally shook him to his core when one of those lights turned red. None of the ones which had turned red had returned to green, so that told him more than he wanted to know.

Elliott put his monitoring system on auto-pilot to record data and set the alarm to notify him in his quarters if a major update came in. Just as he and Margaret were drifting off to sleep ... minus earplugs for the first time in days ... his alarm went off on the bedside table.   .

CHAPTER 55

Elliott went across the hall to what had once been his work room but now was also considered the command and communications center for the compound. The equipment in this room was their only link to the outside world.

He touched the fingerprint ID pad and opened the door to see a bulletin crawling across the red screen. It was on the Emergency Broadcast System and he knew the color codes ... green screen for updates ... red screen for a new report. He lowered himself slowly into his seat and hit the reset button. He quickly glanced at the weather radar monitor ... the blizzard was the same configuration and the forecast couldn't get worse than it already was. God forbid this was something new added to the desperate crisis he and the others were facing. The message had reset to the beginning and he read as the words snaked across the screen.

EMERGENCY BROADCAST SYSTEM ALERT: SEISMOLOGISTS IN WYOMING ARE REPORTING A MAJOR INCREASE IN THE INTENSITY OF VOLCANIC ACTIVITY COMING FROM BENEATH YELLOWSTONE NATIONAL PARK, LOCATED IN SOUTHERN MONTANA AND NORTHWEST WYOMING. IF IT CONTINUES ON ITS PRESENT COURSE, AN ERUPTION OF MAJOR PROPORTIONS IS LIKELY TO OCCUR WITHIN THE NEXT TWELVE HOURS. MANDATORY EVACUATION OF AN AREA 100 MILES SURROUNDING THE YELLOWSTONE NATIONAL PARK HAS TAKEN PLACE. ALL EVACUEES

ARE BEING ADVISED TO SEEK SHELTER AS FAR AWAY AS POSSIBLE. THE STATES OF OREGON, IDAHO AND WASHINGTON HAVE PREPARED A LIST OF SHELTERS AND WHAT THEY CAN ACCOMMODATE. UPDATES WILL BE FORTHCOMING FROM THE DEPARTMENT OF INTERIOR AND FEMA. SHELTER LOCATIONS ARE AS FOLLOWS: ...

Elliott swivelled his seat around so that he didn't have to read any more and could focus his thoughts on the impact such an event would have on the compounds. He allowed himself some time to step out of his role at the compound, buried his face in his arms folded on the desk and sobbed. The adrenaline had been running full throttle for days and he didn't know how much he had left to give ... but what were the alternatives? None.

He hated being the designated bearer of bad news. The worst forecast he had ever been called on to give was of a Category 3 hurricane in Florida. Its predicted path had been from Miami to Ft. Myers ... far south of Jacksonville. He had never even been in a hurricane ... or tornado ... and now he was part of the entire country which appeared to be heading for Doomsday. He knew the average citizen had no idea what the implications were of a full eruption of Yellowstone. He wished he was one of them at that point, living in blissful ignorance of the demon beneath the ground that could destroy humanity ... and take a long time to do it.

BLACK SNOW ... by Anne Rushton

None of the compounds had been located in the western half of the country. They expected the need to be greater in the eastern half because of hurricanes ... blizzards ... continual shoreline erosion from melting glaciers, an earthquake from the New Madrid fault line at the intersection of Missouri, Kentucky, Tennessee and Arkansas ... terrorist activity near the nation's capital.

Although the hour was very late, he called Samuel. "This is Elliott ... can I come to see you?"

"Now?"

"Now."

"What is this about Elliott?"

"I need you to help me ... get out your Bible."

"Sure ... come now."

Samuel opened his door a crack waiting to let Elliott in and not to disturb the others who were sleeping. "Elliott you look awful ... you're sweating and shaking ... what happened or is about to happen?"

"I need you to read and interpret the Book Of Revelation in the Bible to me."

"At this hour? What in God's holy name is going on? I have a private stash of wine for sacramental use ... do you want some to settle yourself down?"

"No ... thank you anyway and your secret is safe with me ... please ..."

"Elliott you are close to hysteria ... let's pray."

BLACK SNOW ... by Anne Rushton

Samuel grabbed Elliott's shaking hands and led him to a seat ... Samuel dropped to his knees to pray.

Elliott calmed himself enough to listen to what Samuel was going to read. Samuel picked up his Bible and began reading from the Book Of Revelation, stopping at times to explain or interpret. Elliott listened intently ... Samuel's rhythmic reading washed over him like a cool breeze. When Samuel came to the part about fire in the sky and strong winds, Elliott stopped him. "Enough."

Samuel closed the Bible and sat back in his chair waiting for Elliott to say something. Once he started, he very carefully and calmly laid out what was happening at Yellowstone and the consequences such an eruption would have on the entire world. "How long have you known about this?"

"I knew about minor seismic activity since before we came to the compound but I didn't put it in any of my reports, thinking there was no use sounding the alarm unless or until it was necessary. Besides, sounding the alarm was like delivering a death sentence. I can't imagine how the government or any of its departments are going to handle this. Samuel ... there is no escape for any of us. If that thing blows, it will rate among the worst eruptions known to man ... worse than the 1883 eruption of Krakatau. The ash will explode into the atmosphere and rain down as glass shards for hundreds of miles. People and animals who survive the hurricane and blizzard will unknowingly breathe toxic air. The plume will create its own weather system ... mixing with prevailing winds which circle the globe ... and block out the sun. It would take decades for the ecosystem to recover. You understand the implications Samuel? Livestock breathing this air would perish and without the sun, vegetation would cease to exist in the northern hemisphere."

"Elliott, let me call Joshua to give you a sedative. There is no way you can bear any more of this burden tonight. While he is at it, I might ask for one myself."

"We would have to tell him what is going on and I don't want this information piece mealed out to our team. It's better to do it in a group setting. I will go close my office and go back to bed. If I can't sleep, at least I will rest ... I suggest you do the same Samuel. We will know more facts tomorrow ... thank you for helping me."

"I'm not sure what I did to help Elliott. Let me read Psalm 23 aloud before we try to rest ... it sure can't hurt and it might even help us."

Elliott took a deep breath, leaned back in the chair and mentally walked through each word as Samuel read ... "thy rod and thy staff comfort me ... yeah, though I walk through the valley of the shadow of death, I will fear no evil ...".

CHAPTER 56

In spite of himself, Elliott finally dozed off a few hours before dawn. When we woke up, it was raining and windy, but he knew without checking the gauges that the hurricane was slowly moving out of their area. Now to brace for the blizzard. First he had to check the status of the disaster behind the blizzard.

The Emergency Alert Bulletin was still running across the red screen so he closed the door to his work room and sat down to read the crawling words.

... ANYONE IN THE IMMEDIATE ERUPTION AREA OR WITHIN A HUNDRED MILE RADIUS WILL BE EITHER SEVERELY INJURED OR KILLED ON IMPACT ...

As he scanned the maps Elliott couldn't figure out what he was reading meant ... had he missed something ... oh no, then he remembered he set the monitors to auto-pilot when he went to see Samuel last night and didn't turn his private alarm back on before going to bed. Damn ... I have carried this ball all this time and last night in a fit of hysteria, I dropped it. Regardless, he thought to himself, there was nothing to be done either way.

He read the full report, starting at the beginning, and when the words *'began erupting at 2:00 A.M. MST'* he slumped back in his seat, stunned. He caught a few more words here and there *'more than one plume shooting debris into the air'* ... how many and how high he wondered ... *'early eruptions expected to release some pressure, but main eruption expected within hours and continue for hours or days to fully vent the pressure'.*

He turned around to stare at the blank wall and not see the words which could spell out a Doomsday scenario. Remembering the report he gave at the FEMA conference, he shivered when he realized he had given everyone in attendance a prediction of the future ... he recalled saying 'when and not if', never in his worst nightmares thinking the 'when' would be during his lifetime. The meeting was years ... maybe decades ... too late to do anything to turn global warming around.

Slowly turning back toward the screen to face the demon, he read the full warning. It could have been written by him. In fact, he went to his bedroom and opened the safe ... he thought he remembered bringing a copy of that speech with him ... there it was, buried under everything else they thought to bring. Along with Passports and the usual important documents everyone has, this paper told the story and made everything else he found seem useless.

Going back to his work room, he reread the part about Yellowstone erupting and was stunned to see how closely it matched the official report now being broadcast to the country. He decided to read his speech to the group after breakfast instead of taking notes from the monitor.

Genevieve had called everyone for breakfast but first he had to switch channels and get an update on the blizzard ... people would want to know about that forecast. Oh God, if only they knew how futile their concerns were, and what lay ahead. Somehow he had to make it through the meal, if for no other reason than to give him the energy he would need to deal with the meeting after.

CHAPTER 57

Ben greeted the group in the dining room ... he was the last one to fill his plate and take a seat. "Elliott do you have an update on the hurricane and blizzard situation? I hope we can leave the steel shades open for awhile between the two storms to recharge our fuel cells. Don't worry anyone ... we have adequate fuel stored to fully run the compound for some time yet ... and don't forget Winston's water conversion system of splitting out the hydrogen from our water source to use ... the fuel cells run the operating systems and the hydrogen is just a backup source."

"I do have a report Ben and would like to brief the group in the gathering room following breakfast."

"Winston, it is really good to see you back among us ... I assume Joshua and Janice are giving you good care ... especially since you are their only inmate!" Ben's levity was not missed by anyone in the group except Elliott.

Winston smiled, nodded and thanked everyone for their concern and kindness. "I am trying hard to adjust by keeping in mind that I still have two legs to stand on and my life was spared. None of us knows how precious life is until we come so close to death."

Hearing those words from Winston, Elliott was at the brink of a meltdown. Winston was given a reprieve from death and so grateful to be alive ... Elliott decided in that moment he would give the group the blizzard update and then call a meeting later in the day about Yellowstone. He justified giving everyone a few more hours of solace by reminding himself he needed to talk to Ben before just hitting everyone point blank. As the leader of the team, he needed to be briefed first and not blind sided as the others would be.

As the group moved to the gathering room, Elliott noticed the first white snow flurries had begun to flutter beyond the big window ... the first of many.

Elliott began giving a detailed report of the hurricane's status and how it was finally beginning to lose some strength on its way northeast. "At this time FEMA is not giving any casualty or damage estimates of the trail of destruction it has left in its path. All their focus is still on future damage the storm will do. It is moving east of the Appalachian Mountain chain which will take it over the huge population centers of the northeast corridor. Major cities expected to be impacted include the nation's capital, New York City, Boston, and all of New England. Once it moves away from the mainland, it is expected to fully break apart over the cold waters of the North Atlantic Ocean".

"What about the blizzard" Ben asked.

"It is still raining lightly outside from the trailing edge of the hurricane and this will continue for several more hours. You may have noticed when we came in here that snow flurries were beginning to mix with the rain. This is from the ragged leading edge of the blizzard and it will slowly make its way east. We can't predict how much snowfall will occur or how long the storm will last ... depending on its forward speed, it could take up to a week to fully pass over.

"FEMA has estimated that some of the affected areas ... which at one point extended from north of the Canadian border to central Texas ... received an accumulation measured in feet rather than inches ... and in some places ten feet or more. The winds will be significant which will cause the snowfall to come in a horizontal pattern at times. Temperatures at the center of the blizzard have dropped to zero or less due, in part, to the sun being shielded from those areas for such a long period of time."

Ben asked Ethan and Winston if they thought there needed to be any adjustments made at the house to deal with the coming onslaught. Both responded "none that I know of now". Winston added "the depth of our water supply will prevent it from freezing and the pipes bringing it into the house are well insulated. The water storage tanks are contained within the house, so no danger there."

Ben asked if there were any questions and seeing no hands, he said "meeting over" and suggested everyone return to their work stations. "We will convene again after dinner for reports of the day and other weather updates as they come in."

Elliott trailed behind the group and asked Ben to come to his work room. Ben followed and they both sat down. Elliott had purposely put all his monitors on dim so Ben wouldn't be overwhelmed by what he saw as soon as he walked in.

BLACK SNOW ... by Anne Rushton

"I hardly know where to begin Ben."

"Well, just spit it out ... start from the beginning."

"I think the best way of laying out the full picture is by bringing up all the monitors one at a time and giving you an overview of what we are looking at."

Elliott first turned on the radar screen which showed the hurricane's projected pathway. "OK Elliott, what I see confirms what you just reported in the meeting."

He next brought up the radar screen focusing on the blizzard. "Looks like we indeed are on the very outer leading edges of that thing ... by the way, has NOAA given it a name?"

"Adam ... I know Ben ... but I have nothing to do with the names."

"OK Elliott, next monitor."

Elliott skipped the technical monitors and went straight to the real time satellite view of Yellowstone.

"I'm not sure what I am looking at here Elliott. I see rugged terrain and what looks like plumes of dark smoke." After studying the monitor silently for a few moments, without looking away, he said "Elliott tell me this is not what I think I see."

"I wish with all my heart I could Ben." Both men sat in silence. Elliott finally turned on the monitor which broadcast the Emergency Alert System and Ben slid over to read the words as they crept across the red screen.

BLACK SNOW ... by Anne Rushton

Before Ben could finish reading the script, their eyes were caught by the Yellowstone monitor which showed an eruption scientists had been predicting. Both men shook in shock. Elliott immediately brought up the seismic monitor which was focused on the eruption and located in California, thought to be a safe distance away. The needle was wildly swinging from side to side, leaving graph marks no one could misunderstand. The marks created a solid dark image on the monitor and continued in that formation until Ben turned away, unable to watch anymore.

Elliott said "we should feel the shock wave here, although it will be mild. It should reach us within a minute or so. Shockwaves can travel up to 18,000 MPH in ideal conditions, which this is not ... "

Elliott didn't finish his sentence before they felt the unmistakable confirmation by the rattling of the house. Immediately Ben turned on the whole house intercom and asked for everyone's calm. He also asked Ethan and Winston to check the systems for damage and asked the Security Team to check the perimeter for any breeches. He said the sound they heard and felt was from an earthquake in the western part of the country.

Ben turned to Elliott and said, "how does this figure into the equation?"

Elliott pulled out his written speech and after explaining how and when and why he had written it, he handed it to Ben to read the part he had bracketed in red. "This pretty much sums it up Ben."

"Another great concern to scientists are the frequent small eruptions of the giant volcano lying under Yellowstone Park, called by some the biggest 'super volcano' in the world. For decades, the mud pots, geysers and boiling springs have grown in frequency and intensity to the point that the Park had to be closed to visitors ten years ago. Until now they have acted like relief valves to the caldera under Yellowstone. The question is now not 'if' but 'when' Yellowstone will erupt in convulsions not seen in this country since it has been inhabited. All of us here know the consequences of that event. Enough rock and ash would come from that eruption to bury an area around it the size of Texas. The blast alone could be more forceful that one million atomic bombs going off all at once.

"The winds carrying the rock and ash could reach 100 miles an hour and reach the east coast of this country within four days. The wind would become a caldron of hot gasses. Molten rock coming out of the eruption would be 1,000 degrees ... raining down from the sky ranging in size from a house to a pea. The sulfuric acid released would go into the clouds and drop out as acid rain. I don't need to tell you how toxic that would be to anything it touched. The ash would block out the sun for weeks, months or years. What would follow would be a nuclear winter. That could in itself lead to another ice age. What an irony that global warming could set off an ice age. Seismologists are following Yellowstone *closely, but the truth of the matter is that except for evacuating people within a certain radius when the threat becomes imminent, nothing can be done to stop it."*

CHAPTER 58

Both men sat in stunned silence. "Does this mean Elliott that in spite of all the precautions we have taken, all the work put into the compounds, all of us committing our lives to this and other compounds ... enduring the hurricane, bracing for the blizzard ... all that was in vain?"

"The only answer I have Ben is to wait and see. If what we just saw was the major eruption predicted for years, we should have our answer soon enough. There will be aftershocks and some of them could be worse than the main event. I suggest we call another group meeting and just make the announcement of what happened without going into detail of the ramifications. Once we know the magnitude of the eruption, we can decide what to do then."

Ben called the meeting and everyone joined him quickly in the gathering room. Elliott stayed behind to monitor the Yellowstone events and listened over the intercom to what Ben was saying and some of the urgent questions coming from the group. He did a good job of deflecting with general answers, but mostly he wanted to instill a sense of calm. "We came here because of epic circumstances ... they continue to occur, but our only option is to continue in our normal routine of things. Elliott is gathering as much information as he can and will present it at our meeting tonight. Ethan and Winston are checking our HVAC systems; the Security Team is checking that the shockwave did not breech the integrity of the compound. That's why they are absent from our meeting now."

Later in the afternoon, Ethan and Winston came to Ben's work room to report they found no damage; Ben updated them as to what had happened as he did with the group ... facts only without alarm in his voice. The Security Team came in later with the same report and Ben updated them as well.

Elliott continued to monitor the eruption from the California base ... the major eruption had registered a 7 on the Volcanic Explosivity Index (VEI) ... higher than the one on Krakatau, Indonesia in 1883 at a VEI of 6. Still it was not the worst ever recorded. Elliott could take little comfort in those comparisons. He knew that once Yellowstone started, it would likely continue.

After the group gathered for dinner that evening and had nearly finished Elliott's pocket alarm went off telling him of a new update coming in. He didn't respond since at the same moment his trained ear heard a faint distant sound coming from the west. In less than a minute everyone was hearing it and soon the whole house shuddered and convulsed. Everyone fell to the floor and crawled under the table in a knee jerk reaction ... one that would have been of little or no benefit in the event the house collapsed. Winston was thrown to the floor and part of his wound opened. Amber could be heard screaming in agony.

Once the shockwave passed to the east of them in a matter of seconds, everyone came from hiding but stayed on the floor looking around for damage. The chandelier had fallen from the ceiling and crashed into the table. The power was out but Elliott could still see a look of terror in everyone's face. The convex window appeared to be unscathed. They had heard cooking utensils being thrown from their storage and scattered around the kitchen. Everything on the dining table had vibrated off the edge to the floor.

Ben stood and motioned for the others to do the same. "I can't impress on you how important it is to stay as calm as you can. Look around ... we are still safe ... we have some damage, but we are still alive. Drake, pass out the head lanterns for everyone. You folks know what to do ... make your inspections, begin restoring order. Report any damage to me." Elliott added "without checking my monitor, my best guess is that was the final eruption of Yellowstone ... except for perhaps some small aftershocks which I doubt we will feel here."

Immediately everyone went into action, each doing what they could to restore order. Claudia and Jo began to clear the broken dishes and shards of the chandelier. Ethan and Winston returned to their work rooms to make a technical inspection on their monitors, then Ethan went to the basement to make a visual inspection. Drake, Leah and Jamison donned haz-mat suits for a second time that day to inspect the premises outside. Elliott went to the command center to receive and print the updates which were coming in faster than the printer could handle. Margaret and Polly went with Claudia and Jo to offer clean up help. Joshua tended to Winston's wound; Janice tried to calm Amber. Afterward they went to their work rooms to inspect for damage to some of the delicate medical equipment. Some of the vials of medication had shattered and were leaking from behind the locked cabinet door onto the floor. Samuel went to Amber's room to try to console her.

Ben seemed frozen in place as he stood with his arms crossed, staring out the window at the accumulating snow. For the first time, he wondered if the compounds were such a good idea after all. If the outcome would be the same for everyone, wouldn't it have been more humane to allow nature to take its wrathful course ... and not give a few chosen people false hope?

CHAPTER 59

In a few hours order had been restored to the house to the point of safety, if not beauty, and everyone sat exhausted in the gathering room waiting on the night meeting to start. Ethan had done whatever was needed to restore power to the house, so at least they were warm. They all began to take comfort in the most menial pleasure.

Ben had spent much of this time meeting with Elliott while he gathered the dire information coming out of California and from FEMA. Yellowstone had ... with the eruption during their dinner ... had become the volcanic eruption by which every future eruption would be measured ... if there was a future. They tried to decide what to tell the group and how to tell them in the most delicate way. The only thing they finally agreed on was that the group had to be brought into the complete circle of knowledge, leaving no detail secret. Ben suggested that Elliott relate his circumstances of the meeting at Camp David and simply read the report he had presented. Elliott would then tell them it had all come to pass, letting them draw their own conclusions. He knew they would have questions.

The first order of business was to get a security report from Drake. He said part of the roof structure over the bunker had collapsed ... likely in part due to the shockwave, in part by the snow accumulation. Everything else seemed intact visually and from their technical monitoring system.

Ethan said he had found a loose wire in the mechanical room which tripped a circuit breaker and shut down the power. He had made the repair and restored the power.

Claudia thanked those who had pitched in to help her put the house back in order and clean the debris from the dining room.

Joshua reported that some of his medical equipment had sustained superficial damage and some of the drug vials had broken ... but nothing critical.

Elliott gave an update on the blizzard's location and other details about what to expect. He said a satellite closeup had shown the storm had taken out the St. Louis 'Gateway To The West' arch and that it now lay in a contorted mess on the partially frozen Mississippi River. Travel on the River had been suspended for several days before the storm hit. The monorail system in St. Louis was lost as well.

Realizing that Elliott was near collapse, Ben took the report from him. He told the group about the meeting Elliott had attended at Camp David some time before and said he wanted to read part of a speech he had given. Everyone hung onto each word as Ben read it. When he had finished, Ben said "I am so sorry and heartbroken to tell you that what he wrote about is a near verbatim account of what has happened today. Yellowstone National Park is no more. The first shockwave we felt was a warning shot; the second one was the biggest volcanic eruption in recorded history ... here or abroad." Ben handed the paper back to Elliott and buried his face in his hands.

Margaret was the first to ask "Elliott, how long have you known about this?"

Unable to hold back emotion any longer, he broke down and sobbed. Regaining a small foothold on his wavering sanity, he replied "I have seen mild seismic activity almost since we got here. My main focus had been on the hurricane and blizzard. I didn't know about the first eruption until just a few minutes before the shockwave hit us. I knew immediately what it was that we all felt, but I was hoping that was the first and last eruption. Underground volcanoes and their activity are not things a meteorologist involves himself with; that comes under the jurisdiction of a geologist."

Samuel asked Elliott if the predictions he had laid out in his speech were just a possibility or worst case scenario. "Both Samuel, I am sorry to say."

"So you are telling us that all the predictions you made will come to pass, including a nuclear winter?"

"Only time will tell us that. Now we are back into my ballpark because the prevailing winds may or may not carry the ash across us directly." Elliott knew he was stalling for time to allow them some hope. He knew they were doomed.

Ben asked Samuel to give them some hope, courage to face the future, wisdom to keep the compound going, bravery to accept the outcome, and for God to have mercy on their souls ... even though humanity might not deserve it.

BLACK SNOW ... by Anne Rushton

Everyone finally let go of their restraint and Elliott could hear muffled crying from many of them. As Samuel was taking his time tonight in prayer, Elliott couldn't help but think of the irony ... the one thing in this whole scenario that was not caused by humanity was the very thing which could spell its doom. OK, we earned the hurricanes, we earned the blizzard ... but the volcano erupting ... he almost laughed at the thought. Laughter was not something anyone else felt like doing. In fact, Elliott felt he was getting closer and closer to a total meltdown. He would be useless then ... but if all this comes to pass, his presence at the compound would have been useless anyway.

No one could sleep, so Genevieve suggested they gather in the dining room for coffee and a snack ... and watch the snow fall. It was ... at that point ... a poignant scene.

CHAPTER 60

Except for small rumbles appearing on the seismograph during the days after, there was no evidence at the compound of any more eruptions. FEMA was beginning to send out statistical information from the hurricane ... deaths, injuries, estimates of property loss. Even if they survived the eruption's aftermath, Elliott doubted anyone in the house had a home to return to. Satellite pictures taken before dark showed parts of Florida he couldn't even recognize. The only part of that state to be spared was an area between Ocala and Lake Okeechobee. North of Ocala had been hit by the full force of the combined hurricanes; south of the Lake had taken a direct hit by Alicia when it originally made landfall on the east coast near Miami. Everything else lay in a debris field.

The blizzard continued to intensify with each passing hour and day. When Drake had last gone outside to check for damage from the second shockwave, he had the presence of mind to mount a hand drawn measuring stick which he secured to one of the few remaining tree trunks. The snow inched its way up the stick in the days to come and by the fourth day, it not only topped the four foot tall stick and obliterated the numbers, but it was now falling mixed with black ash. The blizzard showed no sign of letting up, but the ash fall had just started.

Elliott continued to track the path of the ash fallout as it caught up with the ever widening snowstorm. He could see that none of the states east of the Mississippi River would escape not only snowfall, but debris fallout as well. Days turned into weeks and while the blizzard was slowly moving east, it had been replaced by debris fallout. The scene outside the unshuttered dining room window was a scene from a horror movie ... as far as the eye could see, everything was covered in black ash atop the frozen white snow.

By then, there were only three compound lights still green ... theirs and two others. Elliott prayed for those two lights to stay green because it meant a sign of life where it could not be found otherwise. FEMA's headquarters continued to operate but he was only receiving scattered reports. The damage had been done ... from coast to coast, north to south except for small pockets in southern California and the strip of land in Florida. There was no way FEMA could remedy or manage a clean up of that magnitude.

Except for these dated reports, Elliott and most everyone lost track of time. They had a large calendar in the gathering room and after each nightly meeting, Ben would cross off another day.

NOAA continued to issue dire reports of weather conditions, which by mid-December included the fact that the debris field continued to encircle the Earth in the northern hemisphere and sulfuric acid was falling out of the clouds as acid rain. None of the agencies would hazard a guess how long this would last. Yellowstone continued to burp or spew from time-to-time, but Elliott didn't bother reporting it.

BLACK SNOW ... by Anne Rushton

Ben and Elliott conferred and decided it was time to speak to the group in a very candid way. Elliott put together a summary report and at one of the nightly meetings, delivered it.

"Ben and I decided we needed to give our team a report ... a summary of recent events ... and what our exact status is here. I don't need to belabor the weather ... the hurricanes, the blizzard and while not weather related, the Yellowstone eruption has had an impact on the weather none of us expected. We came here initially because of the hurricanes, but we stayed because of two things: the unprecedented storm-related damage to the country's infrastructure and because of the fallout from Yellowstone.

"I can't bring myself to think about what has happened in the grand scheme of things, but FEMA, DHS and the White House have all confirmed my worst fears. FEMA and the National Guard are still doing body counts and damage estimates. As you can imagine, most of this is done by aerial drones. The country is simply too big to send teams of people to make visual inspections. They are still in the unimaginable process of formulating a plan of recovery ... if indeed there can be one.

"The figures are mind boggling ... they estimate that about a third to half of our population has succumbed to one or more events. In months and years to come these figures will increase. The population who survived live on small pockets of land which somehow escaped the horrors we have seen, or had their own survival plans or shelters. The entire northern hemisphere is now suffering from the toxic fallout of Yellowstone ... except for parts of Canada and Mexico. Europe and Asia report the same thing. The eruption was of such magnitude that it rose to the upper levels of our stratosphere and except for the immediate fallout we saw the first few weeks, what is left is now orbiting the Earth. Oxygen has been displaced, the normal exchange of carbon dioxide to oxygen between animal and plant life has been completely disrupted.

"There are unofficial reports of people trying desperately to escape to areas which are unaffected ... for the most part in the southern hemisphere. The continents of South America, Africa and Australia are recognized as being the only safe haven from the fallout. The agencies are considering the thought of negotiations with these countries to accept some of our population as refugees. But who would go and how would they get there? And how would they assimilate into a foreign country's social and financial and governmental structure?

"The clean up in this country will take years and perhaps decades ... and perhaps it will never be fully restored. The monetary system and normal cash flow on a national basis has been completely disrupted ... and there are just so many survivors who would be able to perform the work ... and when could it begin? Not for quite some time.

BLACK SNOW ... by Anne Rushton

"In some ways, our country has reverted to the days of the Pilgrims ... refugees who will have to make their own way with whatever means that are available.

"The time has come for each of us to make peace with the thought that if we as individuals are to survive, we have no choice but to remain here in the compound indefinitely. We have about twenty months of food and supplies still stockpiled here. Perhaps during that time a solution will be found to at least restart the wheels of government and food production. Those two things are the most critical to recovery. As a country, we need leaders and something to eat and some way to distribute the meager resources.

"I am not part of any recovery efforts ... my only area of expertise has been and still is in meteorology. I can only report what I read."

Ben stood facing the somber group. Looking around at the faces, he knew that they somehow already knew what Elliott had just told them. Part of their 'Oath of Allegiance' contained the caveat that once they entered the compound, there was the possibility they would stay there for an undetermined period of time. He bluntly asked if there was anyone in the group who wanted to be relieved of their obligation and return to the outside world.

There were no hands showing and even the strongest among them either stared into space or cried silently.

CHAPTER 61

Samuel had a little surprise for the group. With Claudia's help, the week of the Christmas celebration he put out a small table size artificial Christmas Tree on the gathering room table. It had lights and symbolic ornaments from all religions. He decided against adding spray snow or the icicles he had brought to the compound along with the tree. Before the group gathered the first night after the tree had been put in place, its lights were turned on and the room lights were dimmed. Genevieve had made some special holiday treats for the evening and even brought out some candles for the serving table. Samuel had made some other secret preparations. He brought out wafers and the sacramental wine to offer Communion to anyone wanting to receive it.

It was the brightest event the group had had in weeks. In spite of their circumstances, they truly were cheered by the efforts to add something special ... and so unexpected. Ben suggested they dispense with reports, unless someone had something new to add. Seeing no hands, he thanked Samuel, Claudia and Genevieve for such a wonderful surprise. "Samuel, in the past we have allowed ourselves to be politically incorrect more than once, and again, I would ask you to talk to us about your thoughts of Christmas. Read us the Bible passages in the Gospels which retell the story."

"Thank you Ben, and begging the indulgence of those who may be of faiths who do not celebrate Christmas, please consider this to be a celebration of life and a time to acknowledge the importance of traditions in our lives."

All listened intently as Samuel read the familiar passages, shared his memories of Christmas from a child's point of view, talked about what the holidays had meant to soldiers he had ministered to, and finally the feeling of hope the season brought to him then in the autumn of his life. He concluded by offering anyone who cared to partake to receive Holy Communion, another favorite ritual and tradition from his life. Ben was the first one to stand up and lower himself to his knees. He was followed, one by one, until everyone in the room sincerely wanted to receive this ceremonial gift, although some of them didn't know or fully understand it. For two of them, it was the first time in their lives they had been a part of this ceremony. Samuel then summoned God to watch over them and lead them safely to whatever path He had chosen for them. Some of the team wept openly; others returned to their chair in prayer mode; others meditated to themselves; others felt a strange sense of calm they had not felt for a very ... very long time.

BLACK SNOW ... by Anne Rushton

❄ ❄ ❄ *EPILOGUE* ❄ ❄ ❄

The final chapter of this book will not be written by the author, but rather by history. It could have many fanciful endings ... but the subject of the story is much too complex and solemn to be taken into any direction other than the one humanity takes it.

While the story is a work of fiction, the actual events portrayed could occur; some say it truly is a matter of 'when' and not 'if'. There is little doubt we have abused the world we live in. We have disregarded the laws of nature ever since we climbed down from the trees and began to walk upright.

Some say the industrial age in America has been our finest hour; others would argue it has also been our darkest. Stripping the earth of its minerals, top soil, virgin forests, animals for our own selfish use whether it be for sport, food or feather, polluting the air, ground and water on which our life depends. There have been a few faint voices of restraint amid the sea of bellowing screams for more, more, more.

BLACK SNOW ... by Anne Rushton

Nothing comes without a price and so far we have avoided paying it. This won't last very much longer. The debt collector will be coming to extract the price for our wanton behavior ... and it will be steep.

Our greatest enemy comes not from the outside in, but from the inside out.

BLACK SNOW ... by Anne Rushton

ABOUT THE AUTHOR ...

 While **Anne Rushton** is my name ... the one I am writing under for this book ... it is an abbreviated form of my full name simply because it fits more neatly on a book cover and is easier to remember.

My life began in a small mining community in West Virginia ... the area which in the 1960s became known simply as "Appalachia". For those who can remember the 1960s, that word brings to mind a hard, tired part of the country where stark black and white pictures spoke more than words ever could. I was a part of that culture, and in the maturing evolution that eventually overtakes almost all of us, have come to have a deep appreciation of my roots and of the qualities of the inhabitants of that region. Words like grit and determination and pride and perseverance come to mind. In 1980, I left that world and moved to Florida. I needed to test myself away from the comforting circle of family and friends to see if I had what it took to make a life of my own. My husband and I ventured far afield of our roots and all that was familiar. Though I moved far beyond that area in distance, I was never far from its influence. I am an ordinary woman who took an extraordinary journey.

I relived that journey of some 50+ years in a set of four books published in 2013 on Kindle and Amazon. Each book dovetails into the next as part of **The Crossover Series** and were written under the pen name of Micala:

"The Day After Yesterday"
"From Here To ... Everywhere"
"Crossing Bridges And Burning Others"
"In Search Of Me"

The book you have read ... and hopefully enjoyed, *"Black Snow"* is my first novel. I should say it is part fiction, because the subject ... global warming ... is real.

I have been an active genealogist for the better part of forty years and have written seven books on specific parts of my family's history. I have also been a contributor to certain web sites devoted to genealogy. I wrote and published a history of my Church in observance of its 20th anniversary. I am humbled by the warm reception these other books and articles have received.